"You live here here all alone? In this great big house?"

"Yes."

"You're sure we won't be a bother?"

Bending down to grab a carton of milk, Bree hadn't heard Mitch clearly. The low rumble of his voice, however, had sent a shiver zinging up her spine. She straightened abruptly to ask, "What?" and found him standing close behind her. Very close.

Her senses were bombarded by his clean, masculine scent, his overpowering presence and his exhilarating voice. Awed by her reaction to his innocent nearness, Bree wanted to climb into the refrigerator and pull the door shut behind her. Instead, she sidled away and put the center island workstation between her and the attractive man.

Mitch watched her, his arms folded across his broad chest. "I'm not dangerous, you know."

Books by Valerie Hansen

Love Inspired

The Wedding Arbor #84
The Troublesome Angel #103
The Perfect Couple #119
Second Chances #139
Love One Another #154
Blessings of the Heart #206

VALERIE HANSEN

was thirty when she awoke to the presence of the Lord in her life and turned to Jesus. In the years that followed she worked with young children, both in church and secular environments. She also raised a family of her own and played foster mother to a wide assortment of furred and feathered critters.

Married to her high school sweetheart since age seventeen, she now lives in an old farmhouse she and her husband renovated with their own hands. She loves to hike the wooded hills behind the house and reflect on the marvelous turn her life has taken. Not only is she privileged to reside among the loving, accepting folks in the breathtakingly beautiful Ozark mountains of Arkansas, she also gets to share her personal faith by telling the stories of her heart for Steeple Hill's Love Inspired line.

Life doesn't get much better than that!

BLESSINGS OF THE HEART

VALERIE HANSEN

Published by Steeple Hill Books™

STEEPLE HILL BOOKS

ISBN 0-373-87213-5

BLESSINGS OF THE HEART

Copyright © 2003 by Valerie Whisenand

This edition published by arrangement with Steeple Hill Books.

® and TM are trademarks of Steeple Hill Books, used under license.
Trademarks indicated with ® are registered in the United States Patent
and Trademark Office, the Canadian Trade Marks Office and in other
countries.

Visit us at www.steeplehill.com

Printed in U.S.A.

If I take the wings of the morning and dwell
in the uttermost parts of the sea; even there shall
Thy hand lead me and Thy right hand shall hold me.

—Psalms 139:9-10

To Joe, for having the courage and strength
of character to walk away from a lucrative,
prestigious job and come chase rainbows with me.

Chapter One

"If I take the wings of the morning and dwell
in the uttermost parts of the sea; even there
shall thy hand lead me and thy right hand
shall hold me."

—Psalm 139:9-10

Startled, Brianne Bailey froze. Listened. Straightened. Who in the world could be making such an awful racket?

She'd been in her kitchen, peacefully raiding the refrigerator for a quick afternoon snack, when she'd heard the first whack. Before she could determine the source, repeated pounding had built to a deafening crescendo and was echoing through the enormous house. It sounded as if a herd of rampaging elephants was trampling down her substantial mahogany front door. That, or she was being accosted by a psychopathic door-to-door salesman who knew she was there alone and hoped to frighten her into buying his wares!

Both ideas were so ludicrous they made Bree chuckle as she hurried down the hall to answer the knock. "Boy, I've been living in a world of fiction for too long," she muttered. "I'm beginning to think like the crazy characters in my stories." Which wouldn't be too bad if I were writing at the time, she added, smiling.

The hammering intensified. "Okay, okay, I'm coming," Brianne shouted. "Don't you break the stained glass in the top of that door, whoever you are. I'll never be able to replace it."

She grabbed the knob and jerked open the door, ready to continue scolding her would-be intruder. Instead, she took one look at the cause of the disturbance and gasped, slack-jawed.

The man standing on the porch with his fist raised to continue his assault on her helpless door was dirty, sweaty, scratched and bleeding, as if he'd just plunged through a green-briar thicket. He was also remarkably handsome in spite of his disheveled appearance. Left speechless, she wasn't having a lot of luck sucking in enough air for adequate breathing, either.

Her visitor looked to be in his mid-thirties, with dark, wavy hair and darker eyes beneath scowling brows. Standing there, facing her, he seemed larger than life. As if the pounding hadn't been enough, his reddened face was added proof of his anger, although what had upset him was a mystery to Bree. Far as she knew, she didn't have an enemy in the world.

"Can I help you?" She managed to speak.

"It's your pond," the man said, looking directly into her wide, blue eyes and pointing with a thrust of his arm. "It's cut off all my water!"

Brianne held up one hand in a calming gesture. "Whoa. There's no need to get upset. I'm sure we can work things out. Just tell me exactly what water you're talking about?"

"From the spring. Over there," he explained. "You built your new pond between my place and the spring."

"My pond? Oh, dear. Did I do something against the law?"

"I don't know. What difference does it make? By the time we finally get enough rain to finish filling that enormous hole of yours and spill over into the creek bed again, I'll be an old man."

Oddly, his comment amused her. She smiled, smoothed the hem of her knit shirt over her shorts and said, "I imagine that will be quite a long time."

"This isn't funny. I need water for my cabin."

"Which is, I take it, downhill from here?"

"Brilliant deduction."

Certain the man wouldn't appreciate her growing humor, Bree fought a threatened eruption of giggles. "Thanks. I'm trying."

"Well?" he asked, scowling.

"Well, what? I had that valley explored before I made any changes in the landscaping up here. We did find one old cabin, but these hills are full of abandoned homesteads. Surely, you can't be talking about that decrepit old place."

"I certainly am."

"Oops. Sorry." Her smile turned apologetic. "You live there?"

"I do now."

"I see. What about your well?"

"Don't have a well. Or running water. Never have." He held up the bucket he was carrying. "That's what I've been trying to tell you."

"Why didn't you say so?"

"I thought I just did."

"Not hardly," Bree argued. "If you'd knocked on my door politely and explained your problem we could have handled this without everybody getting upset."

"Who said I was upset?"

She arched an eyebrow as she eyed him critically. "Some things are self-explanatory, Mr...."

"Fowler. Mitch Fowler."

"All right, Mr. Fowler. You can take all the water you need from my well. Will that satisfy you?"

"I guess that's my only choice." Some of the tension left him. "My Uncle Eldon and Aunt Vi used to live in the same old cabin. Maybe you knew them."

"I'm afraid not. I'm Brianne Bailey. Bree, for short." She politely offered to shake hands, waiting while Mitch wiped his on his jeans. "I'm not from around here. I…"

The moment Mitch's hand touched hers she forgot whatever else she was going to say. Staring at him, she realized that he was returning her gaze with a look of equal amazement. Now that he was no longer irate, his glance seemed warmer, more appealing. It reminded her of a cup of dark, rich coffee on a cold winter's morning.

Brianne didn't know how long she stood there holding the stranger's hand, because time had ceased to register. She didn't come to her senses until she heard him clear his throat.

"I'm sorry I came on so strong just now," Mitch said, finally letting go and stepping away. "When I discovered we had no water it threw me for a loop."

"I'm sure it did." Bree eyed the bucket. "Before I get back to work I suppose I should show you where to fill that."

"That won't be necessary. It's too hot to come outside if you don't need to. Just point me in the right direction, and I'll get out of your hair."

The mention of temperature and hair together made her unconsciously lift her long, honey-blond tresses off her neck to cool her skin. Even in shorts and a sleeveless blouse she was feeling the heat, too.

"Nonsense," she said. "You look like you had to fight your way through a pack of wildcats to get up here. The least I can do is walk you out to the hose. Besides, I was taking a break, anyway."

"A break? Do you work at home?"

"Yes. I'm a writer." She waited for the usual questions about her publishing history. When they didn't come, she relaxed, smiled amiably and pointed. "This way. I need to water the new flower beds over there again, anyway. Sure wish we'd get some decent rain. It's been awfully dry lately."

"I know. At first I was afraid the spring had dried up."

Mitch stepped back to give her room to pass, then walked beside her as she led the way down the stone steps and along the path that took them around the east wing of the sprawling dwelling. In the distance lay the offending pond. Closer to the house, a bright yellow hose stood out against the green of the perfectly groomed lawn.

"You have a nice place here," Mitch said.

"Thanks. I like it."

"I do a little building, myself."

She noticed that he was assessing the newest addition to the house as they walked. "Would you like to wander around and look the place over? I don't mind."

"I'd love to but I need to get home. I didn't expect to be gone this long when I left the boys."

"Boys?" Brianne couldn't picture him as a scoutmaster leading a camp out or a Sunday school teacher taking his class on a field trip, which left only one other likely probability—fatherhood. The notion of having one man living close by didn't bother her nearly as much as the idea of his children running rampant all over the hills, whooping and hollering and disturbing the otherwise perfect solitude she'd created in which to work.

"I have two sons," Mitch said.

"Congratulations." There was an embarrassing pause before she went on. "I can't imagine coping with any children, let alone boys."

"It isn't easy." Mitch bent to fill the bucket, not looking at her as he spoke. "Especially alone."

Curiosity got the better of her. "Oh? Are you divorced?"

"No." Mitch straightened, his expression guarded. "My wife died recently."

Open mouth, insert foot, chew thoroughly. "I'm so sorry. I shouldn't have asked. It's none of my business."

The hint of a smile lifted one corner of his strong mouth. "It's no secret that I'm single, if that's what you want to know. And I'm not grieving. Liz and I had separated long before her accident. I hadn't seen her in ages."

"Then what about—?" Brianne broke off and cast a telling glance down the wooded slope in the direction of his cabin. No more questions. She'd already said enough dumb things for one day.

Mitch, however, supplied the answer to her unspoken query. "Liz took the boys away with her when she left me. It took almost three years to track them down."

The poignancy of his situation touched her heart. "What an awful thing to go through."

"Yeah, no kidding. I've got my work cut out for me now, that's for sure, which is why I'd better get a move on. Even kids who are used to living by strict rules can get into trouble, and mine haven't had much discipline lately. Ryan—he's eight—says he's used to looking after his younger brother, but that doesn't mean they won't both be swinging from the chandeliers by the time I get home.''

She was incredulous. "Wait a minute. You have no water—but you have chandeliers in your cabin?"

"No, ma'am." Mitch chuckled. "That was just a figure of speech." Glancing toward the mansion, he added, "I think you've been surrounded by luxury too long. You're out of touch with how the rest of the world lives."

She sighed. "I suppose you could be right. I find this whole area very confusing. There aren't any neighborhoods like I'm used to back home. People just seem to build whatever kind of house they want, wherever they want it, no matter what the places next door look like." Realizing how that comment had sounded, she pulled a face. "Sorry. No offense meant."

"Don't worry about it. You can't help it if you have more money than good sense." He followed his comment with a smile so she'd realize he'd been joking.

"Hey, I'm not that wealthy."

Mitch's smile grew. "Good. Maybe there's hope for you yet. Are you famous? Maybe I've read something you wrote."

Delayed reaction but predictable questions? "I doubt that. I write women's fiction. And I didn't get rich doing it. My father passed away several years ago, and I inherited a bundle. After that, I left Pennsylvania and moved down here to Arkansas to get away from the sad memories.''

Mitch hefted the heavy bucket with ease and started toward the edge of the lawn where the forest began. ''Can't run from those,'' he said wisely. ''I ought to know. No matter where you go, your past goes with you, mistakes and all.''

A jolt of uneasiness hit her as she fell into step beside him. ''I hope you're wrong.''

''Not about that. Experience is a great teacher,'' he said soberly. ''Well, nice to have met you, Ms. Bailey, and thanks for the water. If you ever feel like slumming, just follow this streambed about half a mile. You'll find us at the bottom of the draw.'' He smiled. ''Bye. Gotta go.''

She raised her hand tentatively in reply. She'd have done more, but a flock of butterflies had just launched themselves en masse at the sight of his dynamic parting grin, and she was busy wondering if his last glimpse of her was going to feature her keeling over in a dead faint. The notion wasn't very appealing.

''Phooey. I don't swoon,'' Bree whispered, wresting control of her body from her topsy-turvy emotions. ''I'm just a little woozy from the heat and humidity, that's all. I've never fainted and I never will.''

Besides, *that poor man is saddled with two little*

kids, she added, silently reinforcing her growing
conviction that Mitch was anything but appealing.
Children. Eesh! And the oldest was only eight!
What a nightmare!

Bree shivered. As far as she was concerned, the
man might as well have confessed to being in
league with the devil himself!

By the time Mitch got to his cabin, he'd managed
to spill half the contents of the bucket. Considering
the rough, overgrown terrain he'd had to cover on
his trek down the hill he was surprised to have sal-
vaged that much.

As he approached the cabin, he could hear shouts
and squeals of laughter. That might not be a good
sign but at least it proved the boys hadn't mutinied
and wandered off in his absence.

The minute he pushed open the door, his children
froze in mid-motion, looking as if they were sure
they were guilty of some awful crime and expected
him to mete out immediate punishment.

Instead, Mitch set the bucket down and paused
to assess the mayhem. Ryan had pulled the narrow
end of a flat sheet over his shoulders and tied the
corners so the fabric draped behind him like a long
cape. Bud had apparently been trying to sit on the
part that dragged the floor while his big brother
pulled him around the room. Bud's raggedy old
teddy bear was perched on the sidelines like an au-
dience at a sporting event.

Judging by the swirls of dust on the wooden flooring and the boys' grubby faces and hands, they'd been playing their little game for some time. Their expressions were priceless!

Mitch wanted desperately to laugh. They were just typical kids having a good time. He wasn't about to play the ogre and spoil their fun.

He pointed. "You missed a couple of places."

"Huh?" Ryan frowned.

"That's an ingenious way to sweep the floor but it doesn't do the corners very well. I suggest we use a mop for those."

"Uh, okay."

Mitch could tell the boy's mind was working, struggling to comprehend Mitch's surprising parental reaction. Finally, Ryan's thin shoulders relaxed, and he untied his makeshift cape.

"Little kids get bored real easy," the eight-year-old said. "You have to keep 'em busy or they get into trouble."

"I can see that."

For an instant Mitch glimpsed the child behind his eldest son's tough-guy facade. It couldn't have been easy for Ryan to act as a pseudo parent while his flaky mother, Liz, ran around doing as she pleased. There was no telling how often she'd gone off on a tangent and left the boys alone much longer than she'd originally intended. Still, that lack of responsibility on her part may have been a blessing in disguise because it had led to them not being with her when she'd had the horrible accident that had taken her life.

"I may need you to help me understand your brother," Mitch said. "Especially since I haven't seen either of you for such a long time. I'm not used to having kids around. I've really missed you guys."

"Then why didn't you come get us?"

Ah, so that was what was eating at Ryan. "Because I didn't know where your mother had taken you," Mitch explained. "Even the police couldn't find you. I spent every cent I could lay my hands on to hire private detectives. I'll say this for your mom, she hides really good."

"We moved a lot," the boy replied, eyes downcast.

"It's okay. I won't bug you about it," Mitch promised. "But if you ever do decide you want to talk about anything that happened while you were gone, I'm willing to listen, okay?"

"Yeah. Sure."

Mitch would have pursued the subject if there hadn't been a strange scratching noise at the door. He immediately assumed it was a marauding raccoon or possum, but before he had time to warn the boys, Bud had run to the door and thrown it wide open.

"Don't!"

Mitch started to shout, then stopped, startled, when he realized their visitor was a puppy. At least

he thought it was. There was so much mud and so
many leaves and twigs stuck in its dull brown coat
that its age wasn't the only thing in question.

Mitch's protective instincts came to the fore.
"Close the door. You don't know where that thing
has been. It could be sick."

The advice came too late. Bud was already on
his knees beside the pitiful little dog, and Ryan was
patting it on the head while it shook and whimpered. Whether Mitch approved or not, it looked
like his boys had themselves a pet.

He strode quickly to the doorway and scooped
up the skinny pup so he could look it over. Poor
thing. He could feel every one of its ribs beneath
the matted fur. Chances were good it was covered
with fleas, too. If any stray ever needed a home,
this one sure did.

"Okay. First things first," he said firmly. "Ryan,
you grab a rag and wipe down all the furniture with
clean water from the bucket. Bud, you help him.
And do a good job of it, guys, because you'll only
get one chance. As soon as you're done we're going
to use the rest of the wash water to give this dog a
bath."

Hearing the boys' mutual intake of breath he
added, "That is, if you want it to live inside with
us. Of course, if you don't..."

"We do!" Ryan shouted. Grabbing Bud by the
hand, he hurried him off with a breathless com-

mand, "Come on," leaving Mitch and the dog behind.

"You guys found him. What do you want to name him?" Mitch called after them.

Bud grabbed Ryan's arm and leaned close to whisper in his ear.

Ryan nodded sagely. "Barney."

Bud agreed, "Yeah!"

At the shrill sound of their voices the little dog's trembling increased. Mitch felt so sorry for it, he held it closer in spite of its dirty coat. "Shush. You're scaring him."

They immediately quieted down, looking at their father with awe. In their eyes, he had apparently become an instant expert on dogs.

Soberly, Mitch gazed at the skinny, quivering ball of filthy fur he was cradling in his arms, hoping with all his heart that he'd be wise enough, caring enough, to salvage all three of the neglected waifs he was now responsible for.

Chapter Two

With darkness came a midsummer thunderstorm. Mitch figured out how hard it was raining by listening to the torrent pounding against the peaked tin roof and running off the steep slope to fall in a solid sheet of water along both sides.

Before long, he felt a drop hit him on the head. It didn't startle him because he was already wide awake. As soon as the thunder and lightning had started, Bud had climbed into his bed with him, stuffed bear and all. That wasn't so bad until a wide-eyed Ryan showed up carrying a battery-powered lantern and their new dog.

"Barney is scared, too," the eight-year-old said. "Can we get in bed with you?"

"Sure." Mitch scooted over as far as he could

to make room and promptly fell off the narrow mattress onto the floor with a thump and an ouch.

That brought giggles from the boys.

"Tell you what," he said, raising himself up to peer over the edge of the bed, "how about we put a couple of these beds together to make one bigger one? Then we can all sleep close without pushing your poor daddy onto the floor."

No one answered. Mitch got to his feet and took charge. "Okay. Everybody out. The roof is leaking over here, and I don't know how much worse the rain will get, so the first thing we're going to do is move my bed to a drier place." He motioned. "Ryan, you push the foot of the bed in that direction. I'll get the end with the headboard."

"I have to go potty," Bud announced.

"In a minute," Mitch promised. "Right now we're getting Daddy's bed out of the way so it won't get wet."

Ryan shot him a knowing look. "That's not the only thing that'll be wet if you don't take him to the bathroom. When he says he has to go, he has to go."

"Okay, okay."

It suddenly occurred to Mitch that the facilities were outside and it was pouring. He glanced at Ryan. The boy was sporting a sly grin.

Mitch frowned. "Did you take your brother to the outhouse before dark, like I told you?"

"Yup." Ryan's eyes twinkled with mischief. "But he'd never seen one before. He was scared to go in."

"Why didn't you go in with him?"

"It was too crowded." His smile spread from ear to ear. "Guess you'll have to make the trip, huh?"

Mitch sighed, vowing to add a portable commode to the list of supplies he intended to get the next time he drove into town. He reached for his jeans and pulled them on over his pajamas, then slid his bare feet into his boots. "I guess I will. Help your brother put his shoes on."

He grabbed a waterproof plastic poncho, slung it over his head and held the front part out of the way while he hoisted his youngest son in his arms and covered him with it.

"I'll take Bud now. Ryan, you fix the beds while I'm gone. When I come back I'll help you. Okay?"

Ryan nodded compliantly.

Looking terribly smug, he handed his father a flashlight.

The humidity gathering beneath the plastic gear had already brought up beads of sweat on Mitch's forehead.

The moment Ryan opened the door for him, the rain gusted in, soaking the floorboards and puddling on the uneven surface. Lightning illuminated the yard as if a floodlight had been turned on. Thunder crashed and rolled, echoing across the hills.

If Mitch hadn't been obliged to make a mad dash for the outhouse he would have stopped then and there and told his eldest son a few things about following orders in the future. As it was, he figured he would be doing well to keep his balance and get there and back in one piece. Discipline would have to wait.

From her second-story vantage point, Bree could see the recently dug pond that had caused her new neighbor such consternation. Every time there was a flash of lightning the water level looked higher. If this deluge kept up, the creek he'd mentioned was probably going to start flowing again very soon.

"I think I'll still run a pipe from our well so they'll have decent drinking water all the time," she told herself. "That's only fair." Besides, doing that would keep the neighbors from disturbing her solitude by hiking up the hill to fetch water day after day. She made a disgusted face. Did having an ulterior motive cancel out the benefits of doing a good deed? "I sure hope not."

As she watched, the water level in the pond continued to rise, then appeared to stabilize even though the rain was still coming down hard. Her brow furrowed, and she peered into the darkness, hoping for another bright burst so she could see better. When it did finally come, she could have sworn there was less water in the pond than before. How strange.

Puzzled, she watched the anomaly for a few more minutes, then pulled a light cotton robe over her nightgown and went downstairs to make sure her computer was disconnected in case of a lightning strike. There wasn't much point in going back to bed while the storm raged. She'd never be able to sleep when the flashes were so bright she could see them through her closed eyelids!

Bree got herself a glass of milk and settled into a chair at the kitchen table. She noticed that her hands were trembling slightly. Undue concern during bad weather was a new phenomenon for her. There seemed to be something particularly disconcerting about the ferocity of Arkansas summer storms. Maybe it was the stories her part-time housekeeper, Emma, had told about that kind of weather spawning tornadoes. Or maybe it was simply the fact that Bree was alone in the enormous house with no one to talk to. Most of the time, that was exactly how she wanted it. Tonight, however, she almost wished it was time for Emma to drive out from Serenity and clean the place again.

Thunder rattled the windows. Bree winced. "Guess I'm not much of a country girl," she murmured. "I'd sure like to ask somebody a few questions right about now."

Mitch had pulled on his leather boots without lacing them, and they were totally soaked. Thanks to the blowing rain and stifling humidity, the rest of him wasn't much drier.

Bud had obviously never had to rough it before. Consequently, their foray into the storm had taken far longer than Mitch had anticipated.

By the time he returned Bud to the cabin, Mitch was furious with Ryan. Pulling off his slicker, he glared at the boy. "You knew this would happen, didn't you?"

"I didn't know it was going to rain," Ryan answered, acting subdued under his father's ire. "It's not my fault this place is a dump. It's worse than going to camp. At least they had the bathrooms in the same building."

"You went to camp?"

"Yeah. Once. Mom sent us. I didn't like it much."

"No doubt." Mitch noticed that Ryan was fidgeting more than usual. Since the sound of running, dripping water had been serenading them for hours, he suspected the power of suggestion was getting to Ryan the same way it already had to Bud.

"You wouldn't happen to have to use the bathroom, too, would you?" Mitch asked with a slow drawl.

"Me? Naw."

"You sure? I could lend you my poncho. You wouldn't get too wet."

Ryan eyed him with obvious misgivings. "You mean you wouldn't come with me?"

"Nope. One of us has to stay in here and watch your brother. If you go, that means I stay." He could see the indecisiveness in his son's face turn to stubborn resolve.

"Fine. Gimme the raincoat. I'm out of here."

Mitch watched him don the man-size slicker and pick up the flashlight. The only thing that hinted at anxiety was a slight pause in Ryan's stride as he opened the door and faced the storm. Then he slammed the door and was gone.

The kid has guts, Mitch told himself with pride. He hadn't been nearly that brave when he was only eight. Of course, he hadn't been compelled to care for a younger sibling, either. That responsibility had undoubtedly forced Ryan to grow up way before his time—which was a real shame. If possible, Mitch was going to teach the poor kid to enjoy being a child again.

Warmer thoughts of Ryan had just about blotted out the last of Mitch's rancor when the door burst open and his son ran in, shouting, "Look out! It's a flood!"

If it hadn't been for the wild look in his son's eyes, Mitch might have doubted his truthfulness. Instead, he joined him at the door and shined the flashlight on the yard to assess the situation for himself.

"It's just runoff water," Mitch assured the frightened boy. "Nothing to worry about."

Ryan grabbed the light and pointed it toward the creek bed. "Oh, yeah? How about over there?"

"That's just…" Reality struck, bringing Mitch's heart to his throat and making his pulse race. He whispered, "Dear God."

"You told me not to cuss."

"That wasn't a curse. See the debris in the water? Those are whole trees, not twigs. I didn't know it was raining hard enough to do that." He whirled. "Come on. We're getting out of here. Follow me. I'll get Bud."

"Want your raincoat?" Ryan held it out.

"Forget it. I'd rather be wet than get caught by that water coming down the canyon."

Mitch scooped up his youngest son and ran for the front door. Bud immediately started to bawl.

Racing toward the car, Mitch belatedly realized

that Ryan wasn't right behind him. He tossed Bud into the back seat and was about to return to the house for his other son when Ryan appeared, leaning into the wind and struggling to make headway through the pelting rain.

"Had to stop and get the bear," the boy shouted.

Mitch was already standing in mud and water up to his ankles. Fortunately, Ryan was able to get the passenger door open without his help.

Sliding behind the wheel, Mitch leaned over and pulled Ryan into the car beside him, then started the motor while the boy struggled to shut the heavy door against the force of the gale.

"Where's the dog? Who's got the dog?" Mitch shouted over the combined furor of the storm and his upset children.

"I don't know," Ryan hollered back. "Want me to go see?"

"No. Stay right where you are. I'll get him."

The moment Mitch opened the driver's door the soggy little dog jumped in, bounded across his feet and scrambled over the back of the front seat as if he'd always done it that way.

The boys cheered.

"Belt yourselves in!" Mitch ordered.

He put the car in reverse, praying the tires wouldn't slip in the slimy mud and wishing he'd had enough foresight to bring his four-wheel-drive pickup truck instead of the cumbersome passenger car.

Gently, evenly, he pressed the accelerator. Every instinct screamed for him to gun the motor, to race onto the paved road as fast as he could. But he knew better than to try.

The rear wheels slipped, spun. Mitch eased up on the gas, and they finally caught. He prayed a silent thanks to his heavenly Father, then added a fervent, soul-deep plea for further help, just as he had every single day and night his sons had been missing. Nothing like a disaster to bring out the spiritual side of a man, was there? Well, at least *something* good had come out of that time of horrible worry and loneliness.

Mitch's hands clenched the wheel.

The heavy vehicle slipped and slid in and out of ruts as it inched backward out of the valley.

Even if there had been room to turn the car around, he wouldn't have tried the maneuver in this weather. Too much chance of going off the road and getting mired in one of the ditches that ran along both sides.

He hardly had time to think about that danger before they skidded off the road and were mired up to their axles! Terrific. Now what? He glanced at his sons.

Ryan gave him a cynical look in reply. "Smooth move, Dad."

Under other circumstances Mitch would have countered that comment, but right now he had more important things on his mind than the boy's pessimism. He had to decide quickly what to do with his wet, shivering kids and the soggy dog. Given the current conditions, staying in the car was out of the question.

It didn't take a genius to see that a short hike to the estate up the hill was the only sensible course of action. For the sake of the kids, he'd have to swallow his pride and ask for help. Again.

Too bad he hadn't tried to make a better impression on the wealthy woman who lived there the first time he'd knocked on her door.

Getting Bud and Ryan up the hill was a lot harder for Mitch than climbing with the bucket had been. It was also dark and wet, and everybody was clammy and slippery.

Mitch finally slung the smaller boy under one arm like a sack of potatoes so he could carry him and still have one hand free to grab low-hanging tree branches to aid his ascent.

Ryan tried valiantly to keep up but made little forward progress while he was trying to hold on to the soggy dog. Finally, he set Barney down to fend for himself and concentrated on toting only the drenched teddy bear while Mitch struggled along with Bud.

By the time they topped the rise and came out of the forest onto the lawn of the estate, Mitch was so exhausted he dropped to his knees.

Fighting to catch his breath, he set Bud on his feet, "Okay. You can walk now."

Though the rain had slackened some, it was still falling. Gusting wind made it feel colder. He pointed toward the house, thankful a few lights were on inside so the boys could see it clearly. "That's where we're going. It's not much farther."

Ryan drew up beside his father and whistled. "Whoa. Cool. Why didn't you bring us here in the first place?"

"Look, the only reason we're here tonight is because we need shelter and a dry place to sleep," Mitch explained. "In the morning we'll head back down to the cabin and see what kind of shape it's in."

"Bummer."

"Get over it." Mitch stood. "Come on, fellas. I don't know about you, but I'm freezing. Grab the dog and let's go."

Chapter Three

Brianne was still sitting in the kitchen when she thought she heard a knock on the front door. Chalking it up to her imagination, she didn't move. As isolated as the house was, she hardly ever had company, even on a nice day. On a wretched night like this it was unheard of.

A second knock made her jump. "Who in the world can that be?" There was only one way to find out—answer the door. But what if it was a burglar?

"A burglar wouldn't knock," she countered, chuckling softly. Just in case, however, she'd leave the chain fastened till she saw who it was. Too bad she didn't have a baseball bat handy.

"Sure, then if it is a burglar I can ask him if he wants to play a few innings?" Bree taunted herself.

She was still smiling at the amusing idea as she unlocked the front door and opened it far enough to see if she really did have callers.

Oh, my! She certainly did! Not only was Mitch Fowler standing on her porch big as life—he had two dripping wet children at his side. The pose reminded her of a mother hen corralling her chicks to shelter them beneath her wings. How adorable!

Brianne quickly undid the chain and threw the door wide. "You look awful. Get in here where it's dry."

"You sure?"

"Of course!"

"Thanks. We got flooded out, and I didn't know where else to go. The kids are pretty cold."

Ushering his boys through the door without delay, he ran his hands over his wet hair to smooth it back, apparently trying to make himself presentable.

Bree thought he looked absolutely endearing. The tender way he was hovering over his children touched her heart and created a never-to-be-forgotten picture of true parenting. When she was little she would have given anything to see that kind of love in her father's expression. The thought brought a melancholy smile.

Mitch's glance met hers and lingered. "I hate to be a bother. Have you got a couple of extra blankets we could borrow? And maybe some spare towels?"

"Of course." Blushing and pulling her cotton robe around her more tightly, she said, "Stay right where you are. Don't move. I'll go get them."

She frowned momentarily at the water puddling on her shiny marble foyer floor, then hurried down the hall. In moments she was back and handing out towels. "Here. These will get you started."

"Thanks. I'm really sorry about this, Ms. Bailey. I hadn't intended to bother you again."

"Please, call me Bree."

"Bree? Okay. This is Ryan." Mitch laid a hand on the boy's thin shoulder, then touched his sibling in turn. "And this is Bud. The little furry one Ryan's holding is named Barney. He's new to our family."

"How—sweet." Though the whole group was dripping, the dog was definitely the dirtiest. Clearly, she wasn't going to be able to dry off her guests and then send them packing. Therefore, they'd have to make other arrangements. Ones that would keep the current mess confined to a small area.

"I guess I should see what I can find for the boys to wear until their clothes and shoes are dry. As for you…" A blush warmed her cheeks when she scanned Mitch's full height. "You're much bigger than I am. I'm afraid you'll have to rough it."

"No problem—as long as my kids are okay. We really appreciate your hospitality, ma'am. We'll be out of here as soon as possible."

Bree shivered. The whole idea of having them stay, even temporarily, was so unsettling it made her insides tremble as she doled out more fluffy bath towels. And to think she'd just been yearning for some company because of the storm! What a stupid idea. Being lonesome was starting to look better by the minute.

Mitch's hand accidentally brushed hers when he accepted the last towel. Startled, she pulled back and folded her arms across her chest in a defensive posture.

He gave her a concerned look. "You okay?"

"Storms make me nervous," she replied.

"Not me. At least not until the one tonight. I've never seen that creek by Eldon's rise so high or move so fast. I was afraid it might take out the whole cabin."

"Is that what you meant by a flood?"

"Yeah." Mitch draped another towel around Bud's neck and proceeded to tousle his hair to dry it. "I tried to drive out to the main road, but we never made it."

"Dad backed into a ditch and we got stuck,"

Ryan piped up, wiggling and squirming. "Can I take a bath? I think I've got mud in my shorts."

"Ryan! That's enough. Mind your manners."

Amused, Brianne pointed. "Sounds like a good idea to me. The downstairs bathroom is right around that corner. It has a large shower and linen closet. Take your family through there and down the tiled hall so you won't get muddy tracks on the carpet. If you drop everybody's wet clothes outside the bathroom door I'll see that they're washed and dried."

"Gotcha. Thanks."

Bending slightly, Mitch began to herd his little group of soggy refugees in the direction she'd indicated. All except one, that is.

In order to hold on to his towel, Ryan had had to put Barney down. The curious pup was busy sniffing his way across the foyer. Behind him, a line of smudged paw prints stood out prominently on the highly polished black marble floor.

"Uh-oh. Trouble," Mitch muttered. Then louder, "Hey! Dog. Over here." He began to whistle repeatedly while the children also called.

Barney ignored everything except the interesting scent he was tracking, which wasn't too surprising since he'd only been with the family for a few hectic hours.

Mitch was about to leave the boys and go chasing

after the wayward animal when Bree screeched, "Oh, no!" and dashed madly across the smooth floor.

She was really moving when her bare feet hit the rain puddle he and the boys had left. She started to slide, arms thrown out for balance, looking for all the world like a surfer hanging ten only without a surfboard or wave.

Mitch shouted, "Look out!"

Ryan punched the air over his head and hollered, "All right!" Bud clutched his teddy bear to his chest and wailed, "Barney! Barney!"

Brianne's slide ended abruptly when she came to the edge of the slippery area. She staggered forward and almost fell flat on her face.

To Mitch's relief, she regained her balance in time to overtake the shaggy little dog before it had walked three paces onto the cream-colored carpeting. He breathed a sigh.

The sense of relief didn't last a millisecond. Barney was cringing. Poor pup must have been scared to death by all the noise, and now...

"Careful! Don't scare him!" Mitch shouted. The warning came too late.

The moment Brianne reachéd down to grab the little dog he whimpered, shied and made a fresh puddle of his own. Right on her precious carpet!

Fortunately, by biting the inside of his lower lip, Mitch was able to keep from laughing out loud. Just barely.

By the time Mitch got his children showered and dressed in the makeshift outfits Bree had delivered to the luxurious bathroom, he was totally exhausted. He was also the only one who wasn't clean, which meant he and the dog were probably still persona non grata in the rest of the house.

His biggest problem was what to do next. He'd already offered to shampoo the soiled carpet, but he couldn't even do that much until he got himself clean and dry or he'd only make matters worse.

The boys were whooping it up so loudly he almost missed hearing the knock on the bathroom door.

He shushed them. "Yes?"

"It's me, Mr. Fowler. Brianne. I've looked everywhere and I can't find anything for you to wear. What if I wash your wet things with the other clothes and get them back to you as soon as possible?"

"I suppose that beats staying in here till morning," he answered. "Hold on. I'll toss them out."

"Hey, Dad, can we go with her?" Ryan asked. "There's nothin' fun to do in here."

Mitch was about to deny his request when Bree said, "If the boys are showered and dressed they're welcome to come out. I have cookies in the kitchen, and it's no trouble at all to make up some hot chocolate.''

''Well… I don't know.''

''I'm sure they'll be fine without you for an hour or so.''

Although he was anything but certain she was right, he gave in to the chorus of pleas that followed the mention of cocoa and cookies. ''All right. Simmer down. You can go. But Barney stays here. And if you guys cause any trouble you'll have to settle with me the minute I get my clothes back. Is that understood?''

Two small heads nodded soberly. That wasn't nearly enough to negate Mitch's misgivings, but it would have to do.

''Okay.''

He stripped off his muddy jeans and wadded them into a ball with his pajama top, grateful he'd left his pajama bottoms on underneath the jeans when he'd dressed in such a hurry.

Hiding behind the bathroom door, Mitch peered around it far enough to toss his clothes onto the pile with the other washing.

Bree waited nearby.

He smiled at her. ''If the kids give you any grief, march them right back in here, and I'll take over.''

''It's a deal.''

She was amazed when she saw the boys parading out. They looked positively angelic! Their hair was slicked back, their feet were bare, and the shorts and T-shirts she'd found for them were so roomy they made the children seem even smaller than they actually were.

The contrast between the way they looked now and the way they'd looked when they'd arrived was truly miraculous. The younger one was holding a scruffy teddy bear, which had obviously had a bath, too.

She paused and smiled, assessing the boys looking at her with such expectant expressions. How darling! Mitch Fowler must be awfully cynical to imagine that such cute kids would cause trouble. He probably didn't have a clue how to handle them properly, the poor little things.

"Come on. This way," Bree said, starting off. Ryan, Bud and Bud's teddy bear followed obediently.

When they got to the kitchen, Bree helped Bud crawl into a chair, then smiled with satisfaction. This wasn't so bad, was it? Maybe their short stay wasn't going to upset her routine as much as she'd thought. After all, she didn't dare use her computer during inclement weather anyway, and as soon as the skies cleared they'd all go home, and she could get back to work without any more distraction.

Satisfied, she placed a napkin in front of each boy and laid two cookies in the center. "Hot chocolate coming up."

"I want whipped cream on mine," Ryan ordered.

"Sorry, I don't have any whipped cream."

To Bree's surprise, Bud immediately began to whimper while his brother made a sour face and turned sullen. Apparently, the boys' cute, agreeable phase was over already. Oh, well.

"I like to float those little tiny marshmallows in my hot chocolate," she said brightly. "I'll put some in your cups, and you can tell me if you like them, too."

"I hate mush mellows," Ryan said.

"Not mush. Marshmallows."

Crossing to the table, she dropped several of the small, rounded balls of candy fluff onto the napkins with the boys' cookies. "There you go. That's what they look like. You can eat them just like that. When they're floating in hot cocoa they melt and get really good and gooey."

The children were still sitting there, pouting and staring at the napkins, when Bree set their mugs on the table. "Okay. Here's your drink. It's hot. Sip it slowly so you don't burn yourselves. And be careful not to get melted marshmallow stuck to the end of your nose. That always happens to me."

She sipped at the contents of her mug with theatrical relish, then licked her lips and set the drink aside.

"I'm going to go start the washing machine so you can have your regular clothes back," she said. "I won't be gone long."

Eyeing Ryan's defiant expression, she decided it would be prudent to add, "If you move off those chairs or do anything except eat and drink while I'm out of the kitchen, I'll have to put you back in with your daddy like he said. Got that?"

Neither boy spoke, but Bree was certain they both understood. Headstrong Ryan was giving her a dirty look, and Bud was clutching his teddy bear so tightly it was leaving a damp spot on the front of his T-shirt.

As soon as Mitch was alone he wasted no time stripping and jumping into the shower. Thanks to the raging storm, the kids had only picked up a few ticks on their trek up the hill, but as far as he was concerned, one was too many. No doubt the boys would be itching like crazy by tomorrow. The power of suggestion was already doing a number on him.

He soaped and scrubbed from head to foot. If he couldn't dig his car out of the mud in the morning he'd borrow transportation and run into town to buy something to kill whatever bugs had taken up res-

idence in Barney's thick coat—and in the cabin.
Until then, he'd see that the little dog stayed confined to this one room of his hostess's home to
avoid contaminating it, too.

Mitch was chuckling when he stepped out of the
shower and began to towel himself dry.

Panting, the little dog looked at him with shining
ebony eyes and cocked its head.

"Yes, I was thinking about you," Mitch said.
That was all the attention it took for the pup to
begin wagging its tail so hard its whole rear end
wiggled with delight. "You, and the lady who owns
this place. I'll bet she'd have a fit if she knew we'd
probably brought bugs into her fancy house."

Barney whirled in tight circles at Mitch's feet.

"Yeah, yeah, I know. You're so adorable you
can get away with just about anything. Like those
kids of mine. I hate to have to start out by being
tough with them but I know they need discipline.
Desperately."

The little dog's antics heightened to include a
frenzied dash around the room. Mitch said, "Whoa.
Come here." He held out his hand, and the dog
skidded to a stop and looked at him with clear de-
votion.

He bent to pet it. Barney threw himself on the
floor at the man's feet and rolled onto his back in
complete surrender.

Mitch laughed as he scratched the dog's exposed belly. "Now that's the kind of love and respect I want from my boys. I wish they were as easy to win over as you are, little guy."

Barney licked his hand.

"Yeah, all I have to do is figure out a way to show them how much I care, prove how much I've missed them, and make them behave—all at the same time." He snorted in derision. "The way things have been going, I figure that shouldn't take more than twenty or thirty years."

When Bree returned, the cookies and cocoa were gone and Bud was sporting a sticky chocolate mustache. She could tell the children were fighting sleep.

"Okay, guys. Time for bed," she said. "Use your napkins to wipe off your faces and hands, and let's go upstairs." Thankfully, there was no suggestion of rebellion this time.

Ryan made the choice of sleeping arrangements for himself and his brother. "We don't need separate beds. We're used to sleepin' together," he said matter-of-factly. "He'd get scared if he woke up and I wasn't there. You know how it is."

Brianne smiled. "Actually, I don't. I never had any brothers or sisters."

"Who'd you play with?" The eight-year-old

looked astounded. Mimicking her motions, he turned down one edge of the embroidered coverlet while Bree did the same on the opposite side of the double bed.

"I had a few friends I used to hang out with," she said. "We'd jump rope or swim or maybe go shopping together."

"Girl stuff. Didn't you ever wrestle or play ball on a team or nothin'?"

"Afraid not. My father tried to teach me to play baseball like a boy, but I never managed to please him."

"Bet you didn't even have a dog, huh?"

"No. My father didn't like animals very much, either." She grew pensive. "There was a stray cat I made friends with once. It was gray, with white paws and a white star on its chest. By being very patient, I finally managed to get it to trust me enough to take food out of my hand."

"What happened to it?"

"I don't know. It disappeared."

"Probably died," he said sagely. Pausing, he lowered his voice and added, "So did our mother."

"I know. Your father told me. I'm sorry."

The boy opened his mouth as if to speak, then quickly shut it and looked away.

Brianne helped Bud climb into bed. She stood aside so Ryan could join him before she carefully pulled the sheet over them both. Bud curled into a ball around his teddy bear, his eyes tightly shut. Ryan looked at her.

She tenderly stroked his damp hair off his forehead. "If you ever decide you want to talk about your mother, I'll be glad to listen."

"There's nothin' to talk about. She's dead. That's all there is to it."

Bree could see his lower lip quivering in spite of his tough-guy affectation. Of course he was hurting. He was a little boy who'd spent the past few years of his short life mostly with his mother. And now she was gone. Forever. There must be some way to comfort him.

"Maybe you'll see your mother in heaven some day," she offered. To her chagrin, Ryan's eyes began to fill with tears.

"That stuff's for suckers," he said, swallowing a sob.

Perched on the edge of the bed, Brianne took his small hand and gazed at him. No matter how lost, how far from God she'd felt since her mother's death, she knew she should try to give the child some semblance of hope. "Oh, honey, Jesus said heaven was real. Who told you it wasn't?"

"My mama."

"How about your daddy? What does he think?"

Ryan shook his head. "Mama said he was stupid 'cause he believed all that ch-church stuff."

"I see."

Brianne's vision misted with tears of empathy, of sympathy, for everyone involved. She wished mightily for the words to reassure the grieving child but found none. There was no way to go back and change things for Ryan and his brother, any more than she could change the painful facts of her mother's demise, no matter how much she wanted to. All she could do at this point was continue to offer honest compassion and hope for the best.

She leaned down to kiss his cheek, then stood. "Go to sleep, honey. You've had a rough night. I'll see you in the morning, okay?"

The child sniffled and nodded.

"Good. Sleep tight."

Fleeing the room, Bree barely made it to the hallway before tears spilled out to trickle down her cheeks. She leaned against the wall and dashed them away.

"Those poor children. What can I do? How can I help them?"

Thoughts of turning to prayer immediately assailed her. She disregarded the urge. All the prayers in the world hadn't helped her come to grips with her mother's suicide. Where had God been when she'd been a lost, grieving twelve-year-old, weeping for the one person who had truly loved her? How could she hope to help anyone else cope with tragedy when she hadn't been able to help herself?

The only positive thing was what Ryan had said about his father. If Mitch Fowler was committed to Christ enough to raise his late wife's ire, that was a definite plus. At least he'd be able to counsel his children based on his personal faith, which was a whole lot better than the self-centered reactions she'd gotten from her father in the midst of her despair.

Bree didn't see the Bible as a magical cure-all the way some people did, as in, "Take two verses and call the doctor in the morning," but she did believe it could be useful for sorting out life's problems, including how best to raise kids. And judging by what she'd learned so far, Mitch was going to need all the help he could get, human or otherwise.

Bree pushed away from the wall and straightened. Though she didn't understand what her part in the children's healing might be, she felt included somehow.

That, alone, was a miracle.

A rather disturbing one.

Chapter Four

Deep in thought and barely watching where she was going, Bree almost crashed into Mitch at the base of the stairway. "Oh! You startled me!"

"I didn't mean to," Mitch said. He grinned amiably and propped one shoulder against the archway leading into the kitchen. "I heard the buzzer on the dryer. Nobody seemed to be around so I fished my clothes out, got dressed and came looking for the boys."

"They're upstairs, asleep."

"Which is where you'd be, too, if we hadn't showed up. I really am sorry."

"It's okay," Bree said.

The only clear thought she could muster was that it should be illegal for any man to look as casually

appealing as Mitch Fowler did at that moment. His
dark hair was tousled. His jeans were snug from the
clothes dryer. And his clean short-sleeve pajama top
left altogether too much arm muscle showing.

"I still feel responsible. At least let me clean up
the mess we made by the front door."

"That's not necessary. I already soaked up the
water. I have a woman who comes in twice a week
to clean. She'll polish all the floors when she comes
on Thursday. Nobody but me will see them till
then."

"You live here all alone?" He was frowning.
"In this great big house?"

"Yes."

Bree hurried past him into the kitchen, knowing
without a doubt that he'd follow. She opened the
refrigerator to check her food supplies, using the
door as a convenient physical barrier between them.
"Do you think you'll be staying for breakfast?"

"I hadn't thought about it. Are we invited?"

"If you like pancakes, you are," she said, leaning in. "I usually eat an omelette, but I seem to be
a bit short of eggs."

"You're sure we won't be a bother?"

Bree had been bending to peer behind a carton
of milk and hadn't heard him clearly when he'd
spoken. The low rumble of his voice had, however,
sent a shiver zinging up her spine. She straightened

abruptly to ask, "What?" and found him standing close behind her. Very close.

Acting on instinct, she held her breath to listen for his answer. If her pulse hadn't been hammering in her head like the percussion section of an over-zealous high school band, she might have been able to hear what he was saying. Not that her befuddled brain could have translated his words into relevant concepts.

Her senses were bombarded by his clean, mas-culine scent, his overpowering presence and his ex-hilarating voice. Plus, his warm breath was tickling the tiny hairs behind her ear. Considering all that, Brianne figured she was lucky to remain standing, let alone hope to make sense of anything he said.

Awed by her reaction to his innocent nearness, she wanted to climb into the refrigerator and pull the door shut behind her. Instead, she sidled away and rounded the center island workstation to put something more solid between her and the attractive man.

Mitch paused and watched her, his stance wide, his arms folded across his broad chest. "I'm not dangerous, you know."

"Of course you're not! Whatever gave you the idea that I thought so?"

"You did. The way you're acting. I had no idea you were here all alone. And I didn't cook up some nefarious plan to steal the silver or kidnap the rich heiress, if that's what you're thinking. Believe me, I'd much rather be back home in my cabin, sleeping peacefully and listening to the rain drumming on the tin roof.''

"I—I'm sure you would.''

"Then if you'll just tell me where my boys are, I'll go and join them.''

He sounded put out. Brianne did her best to keep her voice pleasant. "First door on the right, top of the stairs. There are two double beds in that room. I hope it's okay. Ryan picked it out.''

"It'll be fine.''

"The boys are sharing. If you need more room, the sofa makes into another bed, and there's extra linen on the shelves in the walk-in closet. Make yourself at home.''

"Thanks.'' Mitch started to leave, then paused. "Forget about breakfast. We'll be out of your hair first thing in the morning.''

"There's no need to rush off.''

"Thanks, but now that I think about it, I want to see how badly the cabin is damaged and dig my car out so I can go to town for more supplies. The earlier I get started, the better. That is, providing the rain has stopped by then.''

"Wait a minute. What about the boys? You don't intend to drag them around in the woods with you like you did tonight, do you? I can watch them for you.'' Bree couldn't believe the idiotic offer she'd just blurted out!

"They're not babies."

Oh, well, in for a penny, in for a pound. "They're still way too young to be traipsing up and down hills with you like they're on some lost safari."

"Good point." Mitch considered alternatives for a moment while he searched for truth in Brianne's beautiful blue eyes. Maybe she hadn't been trying to get rid of him the way he'd thought. She *was* right about some things, like the boys' physical limitations.

"Okay," he said, "I might have breakfast here, then go out alone, if you wouldn't mind keeping the kids for a couple of hours."

"Of course not," she said, amazed that she honestly meant it. "They were wonderful tonight."

Mitch snorted a wry chuckle. "Are we talking about the same two—an eight-year-old with a giant chip on his shoulder and a six-year-old with a teddy-bear fixation?"

"Sounds like the ones I met. What I don't understand is how you could let their mother just take them away from you the way she did."

"It's a long story."

"I have all night."

He decided it wouldn't hurt to at least try to explain. "When I met Liz I thought she was the most amazing woman I'd ever known, always fun to be with, always exciting. I didn't realize she was also unstable and flighty. Unfortunately, once she got it into her head that she'd be happier away from me, she was almost impossible to locate. She was too unpredictable."

Even from halfway across the room, Bree could see the muscles of his jaw clenching. Perhaps she shouldn't have probed so deeply but she was interested in learning more about the children's lives. "That's it?"

"Pretty much."

"What about school? Didn't Ryan go to school?"

"Not often. He'll have some catching up to do this year but he's smart. He can do it. Bud was too young until recently, so he didn't miss as much."

"How about getting them a tutor?"

"Why? Were you planning on funding a private recovery effort?" There was a stubborn edge to his voice when he added, "I assure you, Ms. Bailey, I can take care of my family without anybody else's help."

If he had been the only one involved, Bree wouldn't have considered speaking her mind. It would have been easier to simply give up and walk away. It would also have been wrong. Like it or not, she found herself in a position to aid those poor little boys, and she intended to take every advantage of it. If that included alienating their hardheaded father for their sakes, so be it.

She boldly rounded the end of the workstation island and approached him. "It's not what you think that matters, Mr. Fowler. What's important is what's best for your sons. Don't let your pride keep you from accepting whatever assistance comes your way."

Mitch made a rumbling sound low in his throat and shook his head. "Since you seem to have all the answers, suppose you tell me how to get those three years of my boys' lives back."

"Believe me, if I had the ability to fix the past, your children aren't the only ones I'd help."

"You think I need fixing, too, I suppose?"

"Actually, you may," Bree said with the lift of an eyebrow and a wry smile, "but I happened to be referring to myself just now."

"Oh?"

"Never mind. It's not important."

Heading for the doorway, she'd planned to walk out past him. If the overhead lights hadn't flickered at that moment she would have kept going. Instead, she hesitated and sucked in a quick breath. "What was that?"

"The storm is probably causing power problems," Mitch said calmly. "It's not unusual up here in the hills."

Losing her electricity and having to grope around in a pitch-dark house alone didn't frighten her one bit. Having to do it with Mitch Fowler underfoot, however, was a decidedly unsettling thought!

"Everything is unusual here," she said. "For such beautiful country, the Ozark Mountains certainly have a lot of drawbacks."

"That's a matter of opinion. If you had a gas generator for backup, like I do, you wouldn't have to worry about whether or not you lost power."

Bree huffed in mock disgust. "I don't suppose you brought your generator with you."

"It's much too heavy to carry," Mitch said as if explaining to a simpleton. "Don't you have a flashlight?"

"Yes! I know there's one around here somewhere. Let me see..." Turning in a slow circle, Brianne frowned. "I think I may have put it in the pantry."

"Then I suggest you go get it." He looked at the lights as they flickered repeatedly. "Soon."

Bree had traveled less than three paces when the lights flashed one more time. Then everything went black.

"Don't move," Mitch warned. "Let your eyes adjust to the darkness first."

"I know that." Tension was making her sound waspish.

"Excuse me. I was just trying to help."

"I know that, too," Bree said. "You stay put. I'm used to this place. I can find my way around."

"Make use of the lightning. You'll be able to see a little better when it flashes. It'll help you get your bearings."

"Is that more of your homesteading wisdom?"

Mitch chuckled softly. "No. Just plain male logic. Something women don't understand."

She was glad he couldn't see the exasperated face she was making at him. "Next, you'll be telling me that female logic is an oxymoron."

"Isn't it?"

If Mitch hadn't known he was in the company of a well-bred, refined lady he'd have sworn he heard her give him a raspberry!

The sky outside the kitchen windows was alive. Clouds glowed a misty gray, dimming and brightening unevenly as if lit from behind by some monstrous, out-of-control searchlight.

Brianne knew which direction to walk, she just wasn't sure how many steps remained between her and the pantry. Extending her arms in front of her so she wouldn't hit anything headlong, she groped her way toward the door.

Mitch waited and watched as best he could. She reminded him of a sleepwalker being illuminated by a strobe light, and he wasn't comfortable with what little he could discern. What was she doing? Didn't she see the door?

He blurted, "Look out!"

"What?" Bree turned her head in his direction. That moment's inattention was a mistake. Before another flash came to guide her, she'd jammed the end of her middle finger into the leading edge of the half-open pantry door.

"Ouch!"

"That's what I was trying to warn you about," Mitch said. He reached her side quickly, touched her arm lightly. "Are you all right?"

"No. It hurts."

"I figured that much," he said wryly. "Let me see it."

Brianne allowed him to take her hand, but only because it would have been silly to pitch a fit or try to evade him in the dark. "See it? How do you propose to see anything? In case you haven't noticed, there's no light in here."

To her dismay he began using his hands instead of his eyes to survey her sore finger, bring another ouch.

"Does it hurt when I do this?"

"It hurts, period," she said, tugging against his firm grasp. "Quit trying to help so much, okay?"

"You are the most stubborn woman I've ever met."

His exasperation amused her. "Thank you. I do my best."

"You should put ice on that finger, just in case," Mitch said, caressing her hand as he spoke. "The joints might be swollen by morning if you don't."

It was all she could do to continue to sound flippant while he was stroking her injury so tenderly. "I'll live. But thanks for your concern."

The overhead lights suddenly came on, temporarily blinding her. She blinked, squinted against the glare, looked down. Her finger didn't appear to be injured at all, now that she could see it.

Before Mitch could argue, she jerked her hand from his grasp and held it up. "I'm fine. See? Well, I'd better run while the lights are working."

"What about the flashlight?"

"Don't need it now."

"What if you do later?"

Already through the door into the hall, she ignored his question and called, "Good night."

Mitch stood there dumbfounded, watching her retreat and wondering why she was in such an allfired hurry. What made her tick, anyway?

Pondering that thought, he frowned. She had sounded serious when she'd talked about the past, about wishing she could go back and fix her old problems, but given what he already knew about her, her negative attitude didn't make any sense. The past was past. Gone. Beyond changing. Everybody knew that.

Besides, what kind of terrible problems could a beautiful, wealthy woman like Brianne Bailey possibly have? Certainly none as serious as the ones he'd been dealing with for the past three years. No kidding!

Comparing their lives, he pictured her and smiled. The woman had everything—looks, money, a career, a beautiful place to live. Yes, she was alone, but she didn't have to be. She seemed to prefer solitude.

Boy, not him. Mitch knew he wouldn't trade having his boys with him for all the money in the world. Finding them had cost him dearly, both emotionally and monetarily, yet he'd do it all again, and then some, if necessary.

His gut clenched. God, he loved those kids. Being separated from them had been the worst thing that had ever happened to him.

And it had also been one of the best, he added with chagrin. When he'd been at the end of his rope, at the end of his endurance with nowhere to turn, he'd looked to God for strength and answers. He shuddered to think what would have become of him if he hadn't decided to trust the Lord then. There had been times when he'd doubted, sure, but over time he'd come to realize that things really were going to work out for the best.

Maybe not the way he'd imagined. Maybe not as fast as he'd have wanted, either. But they had worked out. He and the boys were together. Life was good. From here on out, it could only get better.

Chapter Five

$\sim$

Distant, shrill yapping woke Brianne at dawn. Talk about a short night! Between listening to the awful storm and worrying about her houseguests, she doubted she'd gotten three hours rest.

She rubbed sleep out of her eyes, padded barefoot to her bedroom window and gazed at the wide expanse of lawn. Thankfully, the rain had stopped. Mitch and Ryan were romping on the damp grass with their dog.

Good thing somebody had remembered to let that little monster out, Bree thought. She'd been so distracted by her late-night encounter with Mitch Fowler she'd forgotten all about Barney. She hoped the guest bathroom wasn't going to have to be redecorated after serving as a temporary kennel.

Brianne dressed quickly, concerned that Bud was also awake and might be running around the house unsupervised. By the time she reached the head of the stairs, however, she realized she needn't have worried. The children's bed was empty, and laughter was drifting up from the first floor. Above the giggles she could hear the musical sound of television cartoons.

Already planning breakfast in her head, Bree went directly to the kitchen and began assembling the basic ingredients for pancakes. Thankfully, the instructions were written on the box of mix, or she'd have been lost.

She'd rarely cooked for anyone but herself, nor had she ventured beyond the most simple fare. If she wanted a more elaborate meal she waited until one of Emma's regular visits and had the accomplished housekeeper fix a big dinner with plenty of leftovers that would last for several days. Not only did it simplify Brianne's daily chores, it gave her nutritious food to fall back on if, as often happened, she got so engrossed in her writing that she forgot to defrost anything.

Now, however, she was faced with feeding a full-grown man who looked like he could easily consume three times the amount she usually did, and two boys who were so fussy they might refuse to eat anything at all. Given those considerations, she hoped plain pancakes were going to be satisfactory.

She had the batter mixed and was heating the griddle when Mitch and Ryan returned from exercising the dog.

"Smells great," Mitch said with enthusiasm.

"I'm not cooking anything yet."

"You will be." His grin warmed her from head to toe. "How's your hand this morning? Any soreness?"

"No. I'd forgotten all about it."

"Good. Can I help you do anything?"

The offer took Bree aback. So did his dazzling smile. "Oh, well… I suppose you could set the table. My everyday dishes are in that cupboard over there."

"Gotcha. I'll find 'em." He handed Barney off to his eldest son. "Go put the dog in the bathroom and wash your hands while you're in there. Then get your brother."

To Bree's surprise, Ryan didn't argue. She arched a brow as she watched him quickly leave the kitchen. "That was easy."

Mitch chuckled. "We'll see. He hasn't followed my directions yet. I need to wash, too, so I'll go check on him. Be right back."

Her instinctive, unspoken retort was, Don't hurry. It was hard enough to concentrate on cooking when she was alone. Having Mitch underfoot made it a hundred times harder. That was one of the reasons she'd chosen to make pancakes. They were simple. You just fried them and stacked them up. No sweat.

She spread a thin coating of oil on the griddle, then poured four circles of batter. So far, so good. Maybe she wasn't going to botch breakfast after all. Hurrah!

It had occurred to her to wonder briefly why she was so concerned about making a favorable impression. Her guests had arrived looking and acting like shipwreck survivors. Under those circumstances they could hardly find fault with her hospitality, even if she didn't feed them anything fancy. So cooking was not her forte. So what? As far as she was concerned it was far better to provide well-prepared, simple fare than to try to make something complicated and chance failure.

The stack of cooked pancakes had grown so tall by the time Mitch and the boys returned, Brianne had put one plate on the table and started to fill another. Mitch immediately went to work setting the table and assigning seats.

"The syrup is in the pantry," she told him. "It's that room over there. Where I hit my finger last night."

Ryan jumped to his feet. "I'll go get it!"

"No. You sit. I'll get it as soon as I pour your milk," his father said.

"Aw."

Flipping the pancakes that were sizzling on the grill, Bree had to chuckle to herself. That sounded more like the Ryan Fowler she knew. The kid was a study in defiance. Attached to his personality, the word *stubborn* took on a much more intense meaning.

"I made a pot of coffee, too," Bree told Mitch. "I didn't know if you liked it or not, but I do."

"Me, too."

His voice seemed farther away and muffled. She glanced over her shoulder. The pantry door stood open, and he was nowhere to be seen.

A second later, he stuck his head out. "Where did you say the syrup was?"

"It's in there somewhere. I'm not sure exactly. I don't eat pancakes that often."

Mitch disappeared again. "I don't see it. But I did run across the flashlight we were looking for last night. It's on the shelf just to the left of the door, about shoulder height, in case you want it."

"I want syrup," Ryan whined.

Frustrated, Bree left the stove and hurried across the kitchen. "I know the bottle's in there. It has to be."

"Okay." With a shrug, Mitch stepped aside. "Show me."

It didn't help that the pantry was barely big enough to accommodate them both. Bree sidled past him, rapidly scanning the shelves and wondering why the room temperature had suddenly risen dramatically.

She brushed her hand across her damp forehead to push back her bangs and made a sound of disgust. "This can't be. Syrup bottles don't just walk off." In the background she could hear Ryan complaining. Mitch, however, seemed amused at her predicament.

"We can always eat them with butter and sugar," he suggested. "That should taste good."

Brianne rolled her eyes. "I have regular maple syrup. Somewhere. All I have to do is figure out where."

"Hey, Dad," Ryan shouted.

Mitch answered, "In a minute. We're still looking."

"Dad!"

"Not now, Ryan."

"But, Dad…"

"Ryan, if you don't…"

Mitch stuck his head out the door for emphasis, then bolted from the pantry with a guttural noise that reminded Bree of his attitude the first time he'd banged on her door. That was when she smelled the smoke.

Her first thought was that the boys had set her kitchen on fire. One quick peek, however, told her that the error was hers.

Black smoke was billowing from the griddle and what was left of the pancakes she'd temporarily forgotten to tend. Mitch had grabbed a towel and wrapped it around the handle so he could move the flat pan off the stove and into the sink without getting burned. If the ventilating fan hadn't already been turned on to clear the air as she cooked, they probably wouldn't have been able to see across the room.

So much for the perfect breakfast. Disappointed, Bree stood there and shook her head. Bedlam reigned. Ryan was screeching. Bud was sobbing. Mitch was muttering to himself and running cold water over the steaming, smoking mess as well as using the stream to cool his smarting fingers.

It was in the midst of all the distraction that Bree remembered where she'd last seen the syrup bottle. In the refrigerator. With a sigh she retrieved it and set it in the middle of the table.

"Leave that for later," she told Mitch. "I found the syrup. Come and eat."

He turned with a scowl. "Where was it?"

"In the fridge."

"Terrific."

"My sentiments, exactly. It probably won't surprise you to hear that I don't cook often."

"No kidding."

"You don't have to rub it in."

"Sorry." A smile began to lift one corner of his mouth. "Are you through cooking for now, or shall I go get the garden hose and bring it inside just in case?"

"I'm through." She put on a mock pout.

"In that case, I guess it's safe for me to sit down." Taking the only empty chair, Mitch proceeded to serve the boys, then pass a platter to Bree.

She took two cakes and handed it back to him. "Can I get you some coffee? I made plenty."

"Thanks. I take it black."

"Coming up."

She'd poured Mitch's cup and was about to add a dash of cream to her own when she saw Ryan reach for more syrup and tip over his glass of milk. He let out a screech that sounded like a deranged owl caught under a lawnmower.

The white puddle spread rapidly across the table, pooled around the bases of glasses and disappeared under the plates.

Mitch immediately jumped to his feet, juggling the boys' breakfasts to rescue them and glaring at his son.

Bree grabbed a handful of paper towels and rushed to the source of the mess. She righted the empty tumbler and dabbed at the milk.

While she was mopping up Ryan's place, a rivulet of spilled milk reached the far edge of the round table and began to dribble into Bud's lap. When he saw that his resident teddy bear was getting wet he clutched it to his chest and screeched in pure anguish.

Mitch shifted both plates to one hand long enough to grab the back of the boy's chair and slide it away from the table. That helped. Milk continued to drip, but Bud was no longer directly in its path.

The paper towels Bree had started with were thoroughly saturated. She held them in place like a dam and reached her free hand to Mitch.

"Get me more towels. Quick! Before this runs all over the floor."

"Too late," he said, glancing at the spattered tile. "Don't worry. Ryan will clean it up."

"It wasn't my fault the stupid milk fell over," the boy argued.

Mitch was about to contradict him when he noticed movement below. He blinked, stared, shouted, "Hey! Who let the dog out?"

"The what?" Bree peered under the table. Her eyes widened. Barney was not only licking up the spill, he was standing directly beneath a waterfall of milk that was splashing his head and back. "What's he doing in here?"

Ryan jumped down, dropped to his hands and knees and went into action. "No sweat, lady. I'll get him."

"No! Don't chase him, he'll..."

The dog darted through the archway and disappeared in a blur. Ryan was in hot pursuit.

Left behind, Bree shouted, "Don't you dare let him shake!"

By this time, Bud had quieted down. He was making questionable use of his napkin, alternating between drying his bear and wiping his runny nose.

"Paper towels! Now!" Bree yelled at Mitch.

His answer didn't sound a bit amiable. "Stop screaming."

"How else can I make myself understood with all this noise? I've never heard anything like it."

"Hey, the kids didn't set the place on fire. You did."

"Only because I got distracted helping you," she argued. "I'll take care of this mess. You go help Ryan catch that blasted dog before he trails milk all over the house."

Mitch stiffened and gave her a mock salute. "Yes, ma'am. Don't throw the extra pancakes away while I'm gone. We'll put sugar on them, roll them up and take them outside to eat."

"I wish you'd thought of that in the first place," Bree grumbled.

Scowling, he nodded. "Yeah. Me, too."

The impromptu picnic took place half an hour later. Mitch had buttered the pancakes, warmed them in the microwave, then added sugar before rolling them up and wrapping one end in a paper napkin.

His children seemed relieved to be eating outside. He certainly was. The less time he was forced to spend inside Brianne Bailey's oh-so-perfect house, the better he'd like it. No wonder the boys couldn't seem to stay out of trouble. Hanging around the estate was like trying to live in a pristine model home without giving away your presence.

Everything was arranged artistically, from the books on the coffee table to the pots and pans hanging in the kitchen. Little wonder she lived alone. No one else would be able to put up for long with her suffocating ideals.

Mitch saw that the dog was starting to wander off toward the forest, followed closely by both boys, so he called, "Hey! Don't go too far."

Naturally, all three ignored him. He wasn't surprised about Barney, but the other two were supposed to listen. Rather than bellow at them when he didn't have to, he decided to follow and see what they were up to.

They'd halted at the edge of the pond Mitch had objected to when he'd met Bree. The first thing he noticed was that Ryan was teaching his brother how to pitch rocks into the void.

The second thing he noted was the void. After the storm they'd had last night, that pond should have been full, or nearly so. Instead, it was little more than a brown puddle in the bottom of a clay-walled crater.

Mitch's heart sank. The dam hadn't held. And his cabin was at the bottom of that hill. At least it had been. No wonder the water had come at them so fast and hard!

Brianne was still cleaning up the aftermath of the disaster in her kitchen when Mitch burst through the door. Startled by the wild look on his face, she froze in mid-motion. "What's wrong?"

"Remember that new pond? The one I was complaining about when we first met?"

"Yes." Keeping her wet hands suspended over the sink, Brianne scowled. "What about it?"

"It's gone. Empty. Your dam's got a hole in it big enough to drive a bus through."

"That's impossible. I hired a professional to do the grading. He came highly recommended."

"Oh, yeah? Well, it looks like the wind knocked a big tree onto the spillway. The water backed up till it was forced out the wrong side of the dam. Without any natural vegetation to strengthen that clay bank once it started to wash, nothing could have stopped it."

"Oh, no." Brianne's heart felt like it was lodged in her throat. Hands trembling, she looked out the door past the angry man. "Where are the kids?"

"Outside. I'll need you to watch them while I hike down to the cabin—or what's left of it. Looks like that water cleared everything out of the canyon. You can still see where some of the tree roots pulled right up out of the ground."

Brianne closed her eyes for a moment and tried to imagine the probable results of an onslaught like that. "What about your cabin? Do you think it's okay?"

Shaking his head, Mitch answered without hedging. "Not a chance. That's why I want to go check it out by myself. No sense scaring the kids if I don't have to."

"Of course not."

His shoulders sagged momentarily. "We must have a real busy guardian angel. If we'd stayed home last night we'd have gotten a lot muddier than we were when we showed up here."

Reading the veiled anxiety in his gaze before he

turned away, Bree knew exactly what he meant. Mitch's whole family could have been wiped out while they slept. And because it was her dam that had failed, their loss would have been her fault!

She dried her hands and followed him outside. "If it turns out as bad as you think, I'll make full restitution, I promise."

The look he gave her was unreadable. He said, "Lady, possessions don't matter to me. All I care about is my boys. Just look after them for a little while and try not to set your house on fire while I'm gone. Okay?"

What do you do with two restless little boys and a hyperactive dog? Bree found the answer to that question by letting them continue to play outside. Unfortunately, it began to drizzle before a half hour had passed.

She called, "Over here!" motioned for them to follow, and ran for cover beneath the patio overhang.

"We can't play in the rain," she said, gathering her ragtag little group together. "We'll wait here for a few minutes and see if it stops, okay?"

To her relief, no one argued. Bud hunkered close beside her to shelter himself and his bear. Ryan shrugged and plopped down in a nearby garden chair.

Barney, however, was not happy to be still for more than a few seconds. Springing off the ground, he grabbed Bud's teddy bear in his sharp little teeth and took off running.

Suddenly bearless, Bud let out a squeal that sounded like a baby piglet abruptly separated from its mama. Before Bree could do more than bend down to comfort the hysterical child, his older brother had darted into the rain, wrestled the stuffed toy away from the dog and returned it.

Brianne smiled at the eight-year-old. "Thanks."

"No problem. The kid's nuts about that bear, so I help him keep an eye on it."

"I can see he is." She laid her hand on Bud's damp curls and absently stroked the hair off his forehead. "I suppose it's natural for you boys to want to hang on to things that make you feel secure. It must be rough coming to live with your daddy after such a long time."

"It's okay," Ryan muttered, shrugging as he spoke. "Not like we had a choice or anything."

"I don't think your father did, either," Bree reminded him.

The boy made a guttural sound of disgust. "He didn't have to sell our house and make us live in a dump."

"You mean in the cabin?"

"Yeah. It doesn't even have a bathroom."

"Well, then, maybe it was for the best that you had problems last night. I'll bet there's something better waiting for you."

"Right."

She couldn't have missed the boy's sarcasm if she'd been blindfolded and wearing earplugs. "Sounds like you don't think so. Why not?"

"'Cause Dad spent all his money lookin' for us."

"How do you know?"

"He said so."

Brianne's stomach knotted. That was exactly the kind of dire economic situation she'd feared Mitch Fowler was in. The probable loss of his cabin and its contents was the final straw. If anybody ever needed financial aid, he did. The hardest part would be convincing him to accept it. As soon as he came back for the boys, she planned to have a serious talk with him.

Barney started barking, then ran and hid behind Ryan. Bree attributed the dog's nervousness to distant thunder, but in seconds the real reason was clear.

Soaking wet, Mitch lunged out of the forest, made a noise like a bear suffering a migraine and threw down an armload of muddy supplies. His face was even redder than it had been the first time Bree had seen him, meaning he was either totally spent from his hard climb or he was even more furious than before. Both theories were plausible. Either was likely.

Ordering the children to stay put, Brianne jogged across the wet lawn to speak with him privately.

"I'm glad you're back. The kids were getting bored. I'm surprised you made the trip so fast."

"It wasn't hard." Scowling, he wiped his muddy hands on his jeans and eyed the meager pile of belongings he'd brought up the hill. "See that? That's all there is left. I was lucky to salvage that much."

"Was there a lot of water damage to your cabin?"

"What cabin?"

"It's gone?" Until then, Bree had refused to let herself consider total destruction.

"Along with everything except what you see in front of you. Looks like a couple of big trees washed down the canyon and pushed the cabin off its foundation. After that, there was no way it could withstand the flood."

"It's all my fault. I'm so very sorry."

The intensity of the rain was increasing, and she paused to wipe her face with her hands and push her wet bangs out of her eyes. When she looked at Mitch he was bending over, picking up a handful of rags.

"We should get inside. Want me to help you carry that stuff?" she asked.

"No. I'll handle it. I'm already dirty, and you're not. But you're right about going back to the house. I've been hearing thunder in the distance. The way my luck's been running lately I'll probably be struck by lightning if I stay out here."

If he could make jokes in the midst of such a hopeless situation, he was probably not as angry as she'd thought. That was a good sign. It meant he'd be in a better frame of mind to accept the aid she planned to offer.

She led the way toward the overhang where the Fowler boys waited. Ryan had picked up the raggedy dog and had taken charge of his brother, too. All were present and accounted for. Even Bud's bear.

Rather than go inside through the French doors by the patio and track mud into her library, Brianne circled to the rear of the house and stopped at the kitchen.

"Leave your wet shoes out here by the door and give your daddy the dog," she told the boys. "You can go turn the television on again if you want, just be sure you stick to watching kid shows."

As soon as she was sure they were following her orders she glanced at Mitch, wondering how to tactfully suggest that he hose down the dog—and himself—before coming inside. Her gaze settled on the muddy rags he was holding. "I'll dispose of that trash for you. Just drop it out there."

"Humph!" He snorted. "If I did I'd be throwing away the only extra clothes the kids and I have."

"Those are your clothes?"

"Yes. At least they'll give us a change. I figured that would beat my being stuck in your guest bathroom again. Old Barney's not much of a conversationalist."

"I suppose not."

Kicking clumps of red-clay mud off the sides of his boots, Mitch said, "I guess I should be thankful he's outgrown the chewing stage. So, tell me where the washing machine is, and I'll start a load."

"It's..." Purposely blocking the doorway, Brianne couldn't make herself move out of his way. She pulled a face as she scanned his full length. "Never mind. You can't come in like that. Take your boots off and leave them out here. I'll bring you a towel and washcloth." Her mouth twisted tighter at one corner. "Those jeans will just have to do until something else is washed and dried."

"You want me to stand out here in the rain? You really are picky, aren't you?"

"It's not picky to have an immaculate house and want to keep it that way. I wouldn't dream of coming into your house if I wasn't spotlessly clean."

Chuckling and shaking his head, Mitch sat on a step and started to unlace his hiking boots. "I don't think that'll be much of a problem for a while. At the moment, I don't seem to have a house to worry about getting dirty."

Chapter Six

Brianne measured the proper amount of laundry detergent into her gleaming white washing machine, then yielded to a strong impulse to add more soap.

Planning ahead while she worked, she closed the lid on Mitch's recovered clothes. The first thing she'd need to do was make a few calls and find him another place to live. Then she'd either offer to drive him down to get his car or arrange for a tow truck to pull it out so he'd have wheels again.

What if I can't find a new house for him right away? she asked herself. Don't say it. Don't even think it. Whatever happened, they weren't staying here. No way. The whole Fowler family was one big disaster waiting to get worse.

Brianne started toward her office while she mulled over the events that had dropped Mitch Fowler and his kids in her lap. The image of having two children sitting on her lap was amusing. And scary. As far as she could recall, this was the first time in her life she had ever imagined herself anywhere near children—anybody's children—let alone rambunctious little boys.

Makes me feel sticky already, Brianne thought. She suspected she'd be finding smears of pancake syrup here and there for months to come, and little maple-flavored fingerprints. How those kids managed to get any nourishment was a mystery. It seemed like most of their meal had wound up spilled on the table, the chair seats, the floor or the lawn. And no telling how much their scruffy dog had gobbled up. Or soaked up!

Having Mitch's family as guests in her home had certainly been interesting. It was going to take weeks to get the place straightened up and running smoothly again. Thank heavens their visit was almost over!

She seated herself at her desk, picked up the telephone and held the receiver to her ear. No dial tone. Hmm. Well, there was always the cellular phone she carried in her purse. She dug it out and began to dial.

When Mitch got himself cleaned up and came looking for her, she was in her office. The door was ajar so he knocked on the jamb. When Bree gazed at him, he could have sworn her eyes had the mesmerized look of a deer staring blankly into the headlights of an oncoming car.

"What's wrong?" he asked.

"I couldn't find you another house."

"Is that all? Hey, don't worry. We'll make do. I've got a little…"

"No—no road."

"Sorry. I don't understand." Concerned, he approached her desk. "Take it easy. Whatever it is, it can't be as bad as what's already happened."

"Yes, it can." Recovering from her shock, she stared at him. "The people at the Realtor's office say there's no road. Not anymore. The stretch between here and Serenity was washed out by the storm. Nobody can go to town and nobody can get up here to rescue us. We're stranded."

"That's impossible."

"Oh, yeah?" Bree held out the phone. "Here. Call somebody and ask them yourself."

Apparently, she was serious. "I don't believe this."

"You don't believe it?" Bree snapped. "It's my worst nightmare."

"Well, thanks a lot."

Thunderstruck at first, Mitch quickly began to consider alternatives. Finally he said, "Look. This can't be as serious as you make it sound. I'm sure we'll be able cope for a little while longer."

"How?"

"By using our heads. All we have to do is set up some sensible rules and make sure everybody abides by them. You'll see. It won't be so bad."

Bree was tempted to throttle him, especially when he picked up a pencil from her desk, handed it to her and said, "Here. Make some notes. Where shall we start?"

That was an easy question for her. "With the muddy dog. It stays outside. Period." She focused on Mitch, and her scowl deepened. "Where did you leave it this time?"

"In the guest bathroom, like before."

The resolute look on the man's face dared her to challenge him. Bree stared back with the same rigid resolve.

Mitch yielded first. "Look. Barney is terrified of storms. He was shaking all over when I brought him in. I wouldn't dream of leaving him outside, alone, in weather like this. The poor little guy hasn't hurt a thing, and he's scared to death."

"Well, you don't have to act like I was trying to be mean," she countered. "I simply want my house to stay reasonably clean. If you'll be responsible for Barney, I suppose he can live in that bathroom for a little while longer.''

"You're all heart."

"Remember, I am the one who invited you in out of the rain in the first place."

"And I'm grateful. Just keep in mind that you're also the reason I have no home. I wouldn't be here if I had any other choice, you know."

"I know." Being reminded of her part in their current dilemma helped Bree gain control of her temper. "I am glad you came to me for help. Now, what other rules can we jot down? How about, everybody takes his shoes off at the door? I imagine little boys love to run in and out of the house. If there's a mud puddle within miles they're sure to find it."

"You've got that right," Mitch said. It was going to be a real challenge to keep this woman satisfied about the condition of her fancy house, rules or no rules. How sad that she gave material possessions such undue importance.

Mitch's conscience kicked him in the gut. It couldn't be easy for her having his family underfoot. And as long as the bad weather persisted there wasn't a thing he could do about leaving, although he found it hard to believe they were stranded. The Ozarks weren't that primitive. There had to be options they were overlooking.

He held out his hand. "Give me that cell phone."

"The battery's almost dead."

"What about the other phone?"

"The regular one isn't working. I imagine the line is down. Why? What are you going to do?"

"Call the fire department and tell them we need rescuing."

"Oh, no, you don't," Brianne said. "I won't let you report a false emergency. If things are as bad as I think, the police and fire departments have their hands full already."

"I never said I was going to claim this is an emergency," Mitch insisted. "I just want to explain the situation up here and get put on their waiting list." One eyebrow lifted. "You certainly can't object to that."

"Of course not."

"Then charge up your cell phone and let's get to it. After all, you don't want to be stuck with us any longer than necessary."

Put that bluntly, her attitude sounded really hostile. Okay, so she wasn't crazy about muddy shoes and dogs with fleas. That didn't mean she was necessarily at odds with the people who owned them, even if she had inadvertently implied as much.

If that truly was the impression she'd given—and apparently it was—she owed Mitch Fowler an apology. With him standing so close, however, she found she was unable to sort her random thoughts into any semblance of order, let alone form a coherent sentence. If she intended to explain without making matters worse, there was only one thing to do.

Marshaling what was left of her willpower, Brianne seized upon the need to recharge the cellular phone as an excuse to move away from him.

"I didn't mean to sound unfriendly," she said, busying herself fitting the phone into its charger. "It's just that this house is very special to me. Why can't you understand that?"

"Oh, I understand, all right. Lots of people like to put on a show to impress their neighbors."

"Being wealthy is not a sin." Bree was adamant. "Neither is having nice things and enjoying them."

"That depends on what level of importance you give to your possessions." Mitch folded his arms across his chest, his stance wide and off-putting. "My late wife had that problem. When I couldn't give her everything she wanted, she left me cold."

"If all she cared about was money, why take the boys? Why not keep in touch so she could collect child support?"

Mitch shook his head slowly, solemnly, and stared into the distance. "I've asked myself the same question a thousand times."

"You must have been frantic. Was that when you sold the house Ryan told me about?"

"Yes. That's what I've been trying to explain to you. No amount of money matters when more critical needs are at stake. My boys mean everything to me. Possessions can be replaced. People can't. Nothing is more important than family."

"I suppose that's true in some families."

Studying her closed expression, Mitch decided to press her for details. The worst that could happen was that she'd refuse to answer. "Not in yours?"

"Not that you'd notice. My parents fought all the time."

"Do they still do it?"

"No, but only because they're both dead."

"I'm sorry," Mitch said.

"Hey, it's okay. My mother took the coward's way out. She swallowed enough sleeping pills to go to sleep forever. After that, I'd kind of hoped Dad would mellow, but he got even meaner. He didn't have Mother to argue with anymore so he started trying to pick fights with me. When I'd refuse to play his mind games he'd get furious and start to throw things—usually Mother's good china or one of the beautiful little ceramic statues she'd collected."

"That was his problem, not yours. Did he die of natural causes?"

"My father died of meanness," Bree said flatly. "He was in the middle of delivering a tirade to some of his so-called friends when he collapsed. They called an ambulance but it was no use. He never regained consciousness."

"Like I said, I'm really sorry."

"Don't be. My parents made their own choices."

Moisture began to blur Bree's vision. She averted her gaze. This was the first time since the night her father had died that she'd cried for him. And she'd run out of tears for her mother long before that. Showing this much emotion was foreign to her. Doing so in front of a stranger was unthinkable, yet there was something about Mitch Fowler that had made her open her heart and bare her most painful secrets.

Sighing deeply, Mitch nodded and said, "This time, I know exactly what you mean. We aren't responsible for the wrong choices of others, you know."

Bree didn't stop to analyze whether it was his gentle tone of voice or their empathetic words that drew her to him. All she knew was that Mitch reached out to her and she responded.

One moment they were standing there commiserating, and the next they were sharing a tender embrace. She couldn't remember the last time a man had hugged her to offer comfort with no strings attached.

The feeling was one of peace, yet exhilaration; innocence, yet awareness; solace, yet perplexity. Listening to the sure, solid thudding of his heart as her cheek lay against his chest, Bree was certain of only one thing. She didn't want to let go.

Minutes passed. No one spoke. They didn't step apart until they heard the sound of approaching footsteps and the clicking of tiny claws on the tiled hall.

By the time the children and Barney appeared in the doorway, Brianne was on one side of the room, and Mitch was on the other.

"Hey, Dad, can we have a cookie?" Ryan asked.

"You'll have to ask Ms. Bailey. This is her house. And put that dog in the bathroom. I told you he has to stay there."

"Okay, okay."

The boy turned sparkling dark eyes to her. "Can we have cookies? Please?"

"I suppose so. If you eat them at the kitchen table," Bree said. The bouncy little dog had ducked beneath her desk and disappeared from sight. She circled to the opposite side and bent to try to keep an eye on it.

"Aw. We'll miss cartoons," Ryan whined. "Mama used to let us eat on the floor by the TV."

Mitch took over the conversation. "There were a lot of things your mother let you do that I don't intend to permit. Might as well get used to it. We're guests in this house, and I expect you to behave that way. If you want cookies, you'll eat them when and where Ms. Bailey says. The choice is yours."

"Okay. The TV's been actin' funny, anyway. It keeps goin' on and off by itself. We'll go watch till it quits again, then we'll have cookies. Come on, Bud. Come on, Barney."

The adults glanced at each other across her desk as the two boys sped down the hall.

"Have you noticed any fluctuations in the electricity since last night?" Mitch asked.

"No. But I probably wouldn't in the daylight. I threw the circuit breaker that powers my computer early last night when the storm started brewing. I haven't turned the computer on since, so I don't have any easy way to tell. That wouldn't be why the regular telephone didn't work just now, would it?"

"No. Phone lines are separate. Better leave your computer disconnected, though. If we are having power surges they could fry your appliances."

She wrinkled her nose. "Speaking of frying, I still smell burned pancakes."

"Are you sure that's not the odor of wet dog?"

Mitch paused, sniffing and scowling. "I didn't see Barney leave with the kids, did you?"

"No. The last time I saw him he was crawling under my desk. By the time I came around here to check, he was gone."

"Well, he has to be somewhere. Stand back. I'll find him for you."

Bree wasn't about to leave the search to Mitch. After all, her office was her personal sanctuary. She looked about the room, chasing shadows. Her random survey led her to the cellular phone charger, where she paused. That was funny.

"Hey, Mitch. Why did you move the phone? It can't be fully charged yet."

"What are you talking about? I didn't move the phone. It's right over…" Puzzled, he stared at the empty receptacle. "That's impossible. Nobody's been in here but you and me."

"And the boys. But they stayed by the door." Bree's gaze locked with Mitch's. Together they said, "Barney!"

Brianne dropped onto her hands and knees.

Mitch did the same on the opposite side of the desk. "There he is! Got him!" he shouted.

"The phone. Does he have the phone?" By the time she clambered to her feet and joined Mitch, he had the dog tucked under one arm and was wiping the telephone on his jeans. Bree's only comment was, "Yuck."

"It'll be okay," Mitch assured her. "It's just a little wet, that's all. He didn't have it long enough to do any damage."

"I thought you said he didn't chew things."

"This is the first time."

"That you know of," she said, holding out her hand. "Give it to me. Let me look."

Mitch obliged. "See? I told you. No real damage."

"Oh?" Bree said sarcastically. "Then maybe you'd like to tell me how to make this thing work without an antenna."

He mumbled under his breath, then set his jaw. "Okay. Don't panic. That can't be our only option. What else have you got?"

"Nothing. Just the normal telephone on the desk."

"I don't believe it! A first-class place like this, and you don't have a satellite connection?"

"Hey, don't yell at me. I never needed anything else until you showed up."

"What if you had a real emergency up here? What would you do then, hike down the mountain yourself to bring help?"

"Don't be ridiculous."

He regarded her with derision. "I'll bet you don't even have any hiking boots, do you?"

"I do so. I've worn them once, too."

"Wow. I'm impressed. How did you manage to do that without getting them dirty?"

"You don't have to be sarcastic. If you must know, I didn't leave the yard. I wouldn't have bought boots in the first place if Emma hadn't insisted I needed them to keep from being bitten by snakes."

"Not during the winter. Only at this time of the year," Mitch said. "You know, you really should get out more. Walk through the woods. Enjoy God's country. You miss the real beauty of this area by not exploring the wilds. In the spring and summer you can spot new varieties of wildflowers every week. Some of them are so tiny you'd miss them if you weren't watching where you stepped."

"Meaning, I need to stop and smell the roses?"

"Something like that."

"Point taken." Bree looked from Mitch to the ruined phone and back again. "Well, what's Plan B? Do we just sit here and stare at each other while we wait for rescue or is there something we can do to help ourselves?"

"I'm still willing to walk down the road as far as I can and check out the damage. If I can work my way around the washed-out places on foot, I'll come back for the boys, and we'll try to make it to the highway.''

"And then what?'' Bree asked. "Hitchhike? That's a dumb idea under the best of circumstances. You're not going to put those poor little kids in danger like that. I won't let you.''

Mitch's eyebrows lifted. "Well, well. How come you're suddenly being so protective?''

"Survival instinct, I guess. I may not be mother material but I'm not stupid. It's miles to the highway. Assuming it's open at all, what makes you think you'd catch a ride easily? And suppose you slipped and were injured trying to navigate the washed-out parts of the dirt roads on the way? Who would take care of your boys and lead them to safety then?''

"When you're right, you're right.'' He gave her a wry smile and nodded for emphasis. "In that case, what do you suggest I do to keep the kids occupied? They won't be happy just sitting and staring at cartoons for a whole day. They'll get restless.''

"So, take them outside and play hide-and-seek.''

"No way. Even if it wasn't drizzling out there, all I'd need is for one of them to leave the yard and get himself lost in the woods. And don't forget the snakes. Copperheads can be especially nasty.''

Her eyes widened in disbelief as she anticipated his thoughts. "Oh, no. You aren't suggesting they play in the house, are you? Of all the idiotic notions!''

''Not a fast game like hide-and-seek,'' Mitch said. ''Do you happen to have any crayons?''

''I have markers.''

''No way. Too permanent. Your rugs would never survive if we let them use ink.''

He brightened. ''How about a treasure hunt? You could set the rules, pick which rooms they're allowed to look in, stuff like that. And we could each supervise one hunter to keep him out of trouble. How about it?''

''Well… I suppose that might be all right, providing we watched them carefully.'' Bree figured she must be getting bored, too, because she was beginning to warm to his crazy idea. ''You could pick something to hide, tell me where it is, and then I could use the markers to draw a map for the kids to follow. I've always been good at art.''

Mitch grinned. It was nice to see the wealthy woman loosening up a little. A change in her neat-freak attitude would be a welcome relief. And the boys definitely did need something to do. They hadn't caused much trouble so far, but it was only a matter of time until their bottled-up energy bubbled over and got out of hand. Like the dog's had.

''I have a good idea,'' he said. ''Let's hide a little

bag of cookies so they'll have a real reward when they find their treasure.''

''Great!'' Brianne eyed the dog in his arms. ''Go get rid of that monster and meet me in the kitchen. I'll find you a sandwich bag to put the cookies in. Emma made a big batch of peanut butter and raisin the last time she was here.''

Following her directions and rejoining her took Mitch only a few minutes. ''Okay. Ready,'' he said.

''Good.'' She handed him a small plastic bag and pointed to the cookie jar. ''Go for it.''

Smiling, he took the bag and filled it, then held it up for inspection. ''Okay. Now what? Where do you want me to hide these?''

''I don't know. Someplace easy to get to but hard to see. And low to the ground. We don't want the kids climbing all over the furniture.''

He hesitated. ''Now that I think about it, this may not be such a good idea, after all. You sure you want to go ahead with it?''

Being totally honest, Bree had to admit the game sounded like a welcome diversion. ''Of course I do. You and I will be right there. What can go wrong?''

He shot her a lopsided grin, his dark eyes twinkling.

''What's so funny?''

''Oh, nothing. I was just picturing you saying the

same kind of thing about your pond before it went south and wiped me out.''

Bree made a face at him. ''All the more reason for me to make you and your children feel welcome here. Now go stash those cookies and come tell me where you put them so I can get started on the treasure maps. And hurry up, before I have time to change my mind.''

Chapter Seven

From her sanctuary in the kitchen, Brianne was putting the finishing touches to her homemade maps when she heard squeals of glee followed by the light slap of small bare feet in the tiled hallway. Ryan burst into the kitchen with Bud on his heels. There was something contagious about his eager, expectant expression.

"Okay, fellas," she said, smiling and holding out two sheets of paper. "Here are your treasure maps. To be fair to Bud, I drew pictures so you wouldn't have to read any words."

She bent over and pointed. "See? This is where we are now. And here at the big X is where you'll find your cookies. Are you ready?"

Both boys nodded soberly.

"Okay, then. Your daddy will go with Ryan, and I'll help Bud in case he gets lost. Let's go."

Ryan was out of the room like a shot. Holding the teddy bear by an ear, Bud clutched his map in his other hand and gave Bree a look that was half adoration, half heartfelt plea.

She smiled at him. "How about letting me carry your bear for you so you'll have one hand free? We'll be right here with you. Promise."

To her delight, the shy child hesitated only an instant before passing her the precious stuffed toy. Touched by his show of trust, she cradled the teddy as if it were a real baby.

"I think we should go this way," she told him quietly, pointing first to the map, then to the hallway. "I know a shortcut."

Mitch wasn't as personally involved in Ryan's quest as Brianne was in Bud's, so he kept his distance and let the boy work out the puzzle alone. All he was concerned about was being in the right place at the right time to keep his excited son from wrecking the place during his search.

Standing back and observing, Mitch let his mind ramble through memories of the past few hours. The more he learned about their hostess's background, the more he could sympathize with her desire to protect her expensive possessions. It couldn't have been easy being a teenager without a mother and being raised by the kind of father she'd described. Thank God his childhood had normalized once he'd come to live with Uncle Eldon and Aunt Vi. It was his adulthood that had turned out disappointing.

No, that wasn't entirely right, he argued. He had great kids. They were both his past and his future, a future he could honestly look forward to. Perhaps that was what had led him to embrace Bree when he'd learned of her loneliness. All the money in the world couldn't take the place of somebody who cared.

Mitch was so preoccupied he barely noticed Ryan entering the dining room. What did catch his attention, however, was the sight of Barney bounding along beside him.

"Hey! Who let that dog out again?"

"He's helping me," Ryan said brightly. "Dogs can find anything. Especially cookies."

"He's done enough damage for one day. Put him back in the bathroom," Mitch ordered. "Right now."

"Aw, Dad…"

"Now!" Mitch's voice was gruff.

"But, Dad—"

"Now!"

The commotion seemed to give the little dog an

added boost of adrenaline. Barking and leaping, he ran around and around the dining room table with Ryan in hot pursuit.

Mitch made a lunge as they passed, missing them both. Suddenly, the little dog slowed, sniffed, then put his shiny black nose to the ground and made a beeline for the rear of the china cabinet.

Uh-oh. Instinct told Mitch to move closer. He was circling the dining table when Barney gave a yap and dived into the narrow space behind the cabinet.

The little dog would have been fine if he'd been able to grab the sack of cookies and continue out the opposite side. Unfortunately, he got stuck, panicked and began howling in misery and fright. The shrill sound reminded Mitch of a cross between a pack of lonesome coyotes and an ambulance siren.

"I'll get him," Ryan shouted.

Mitch yelled, "No!"

The boy ignored him.

After that, things went to pieces so rapidly it was impossible to tell exactly what sequence the events took. All Mitch knew for sure was that the heavy cabinet started to teeter. He put up his hand to steady it, assuming that Ryan would realize what was wrong and stop trying to rescue the dog single-handedly. He didn't.

In the background, Brianne screamed and dropped the stuffed bear.

Mitch raised both hands to stop the cabinet's forward fall, realizing too late that its contents were sliding toward him with nothing to stop their descent but two narrow door frames containing panes of glass.

He barely had time to worry about breaking glass before he noticed the doors weren't fastened closed.

Bree lunged beneath him, slapped the flat of her hands against the loose doors and banged them shut. The clatter was awful. When the edges of the sliding china met the glass, it sounded like everything had shattered.

The front feet of the cabinet shifted toward the wall, then stopped abruptly.

Mitch stood there, breathing hard and waiting to see what else could possibly go wrong.

When nothing moved he took a deep breath, let his temper have its way and roared, ''Ryan!''

Adding to the chaos, Bud had decided to hide under the mahogany dining table. He was clutching his rescued bear and weeping inconsolably while Barney dashed circles around everyone, yapping as if he was certain they were all in danger.

Bree could hear Ryan cursing. She could only make out snatches of what Mitch was muttering in reply, but the few words she could discern were colorful enough to remind her of her father in the midst of one of his infamous tirades.

Clearly, Bree was the only one with enough remaining self-control to make sensible decisions. No one seemed to be listening to anything she said, however, so she gave up trying to talk, pursed her lips and whistled.

The shrill sound echoed off the walls and high ceiling and had an even greater effect than she'd hoped. Everyone froze, staring at her as if she'd suddenly become someone else.

"I learned how to do that at camp," she said, immediately taking charge. "Okay. Kids, get over there away from the glass. Ryan, you grab that dog and take him, too. Mitch, hang in there."

He made a disgusted sound. "No kidding. Where could I go?"

"Good point." Trapped in the narrow space between the man and the glass doors, Bree had a similar problem. She'd created a human sandwich, with Mitch and the cabinet as the bread and herself as the filling. If she hadn't been so worried about saving her precious china, she would never have put herself in such a tenuous position.

"Okay," Bree said. "Get ready. We push on the count of three. One…"

Mitch interrupted. "Wait. That won't work. The front of the cabinet slid closer to the wall when it started to tip over. There's not enough room left between it and the wall to stand it back up. I tried.''

''Well, we're going to get pretty tired of holding it like this. If we need to drag it farther away from the baseboard, let's do it.''

''Can't. There's not enough room to back up. We're too close to the table.''

''Okay, smarty. What would you suggest?''

''I don't know.''

''Well, I do.'' She glanced over her shoulder at the children. ''Ryan, do you think you and Bud can move the chairs away and pull the big table in your direction? It should slide pretty easily on this rug.''

When there was no answer from the boys, their father turned his head far enough to peer at them. ''Well? You heard her. Give it a try. I'll shove with my legs from this side.''

Ryan said, ''Yes sir,'' and tucked Barney into the front of his baggy shirt. Bud did the same with his precious teddy bear.

As soon as they were in position at the far end of the table, Mitch called, ''Now!'' and began straining to help.

The table stuck at first, then let go and slid toward the boys about a foot before stopping.

Mitch sounded out of breath. ''Oof! I hope that's enough.''

''It'll have to be,'' Bree said. ''I can't hold these

doors closed much longer.'' She was losing patience with everyone, including herself. ''It's going all the way up this time. One, two, three, push!''

The cabinet passed its center of balance on their initial effort, paused for an instant, then got away from them and slammed against the dining room wall before anyone could stop it.

Bree's breath caught. She was afraid to assess the damage closely for fear it would be worse than she'd imagined. Even though fine porcelain china was more durable than it looked, it could only stand so much rough handling.

Cautious, ready to react again if necessary, Mitch slowly stepped away, his hands raised. ''I'm really sorry. The boys and I will replace anything that's broken.''

With what? Bree wanted to scream. Do you have any idea how much a place setting of Limoges costs? ''Would you like to tell me what happened in here?''

''It was Barney's fault,'' Ryan said.

A stern look from his father ended his supposed helpfulness while Mitch explained. ''It did all start when Ryan let the dog out again. I told you where I was going to hide the cookies. Neither one of us dreamed anything could tip over a piece of furniture that heavy.''

''Barney knocked it over?''

"Not exactly. He figured out where the cookies were and decided to go after them. Only he got stuck. Ryan tried to wedge himself behind there to save him. I saw the thing start to fall forward. At that point, the only thing I could do was try to stop it from crashing into the table and doing even more damage. That's when you came in."

"Terrific. Why weren't you watching Ryan like you were supposed to be?"

"I was. Things just went to pieces too fast."

"Pieces?" She eyed the mess inside her china cabinet. "You can say that again."

"I said I was sorry."

"I know. It's as much my fault as yours, I suppose. I should have known better. Okay. Everybody out. Leave. I can take care of this by myself."

"Let me help," Mitch offered.

"No way. You've helped enough."

He didn't argue. He escorted his children out of the room by shooing them like a gaggle of geese. Ryan was silent, but Bud punctuated their departure with shuddering breaths.

Finally alone, Bree slowly and cautiously eased open the glass doors to the cabinet. Stacks of dinner and salad plates had slid forward as a unit. So had most of the saucers. The cups and serving dishes, however, were piled haphazardly wherever they'd landed. Some were broken.

Bree picked up a chipped cup and carefully turned it in her hands. The graceful, translucent shape was perfectly accentuated by its hand-painted floral design. This was the kind of delicate ceramic beauty her mother had treasured. The poor woman had always wept whenever a piece from her collection was broken. Brianne remembered her father purposely smashing her mother's favorite pieces, then laughing at the emotional trauma he'd caused.

After her mother's death, Bree had tried to preserve some of the woman's fragile treasures, but her father had found out where she'd hidden them and had hurled them against a wall, one by one, until there were none left.

That was when Bree had made up her mind that she'd never let anyone else rob her of the things she loved. Nor would she ever bring children into a world that could be so cruel. People might disappoint you, leave you, abuse you, but beautiful objects that were loved and well cared for remained unchanged. Predictable.

Sadly noting the cup's cracked handle, she sighed. She'd made it her life's work to protect those treasures that had been placed in her care. It was her way of showing appreciation for the gifts she'd been given, of upholding fond memories of her mother in spite of everything.

Nothing had happened since her unhappy childhood to change her mind about that one iota.

"So, what's the verdict?" Mitch had approached so quietly his question made Brianne jump.

She turned from the cabinet to face him. "Could be worse."

"How much worse?"

"Actually, quite a bit. You saved most of the cups and all the plates when you stopped the whole thing from hitting the ground."

"Hitting the table, you mean." He'd paused in the doorway, his hands stuffed into the pockets of his jeans.

"I stand corrected. Where's the rest of your wild bunch?"

"Sleeping in front of the TV. Except for Barney, that is. I put him in the bathroom. And I've warned Ryan that if he lets him out again, he'll be keeping him company in there for the rest of the day."

Brianne gave him an exaggerated scowl. "I hope he's learned to follow the rules this time."

"Yeah, well… Ryan was trying to catch the dog to put him back when they had their accident. Would it do me any good to say I'm sorry again, or are you sick of hearing it?"

"I think you've groveled enough," Bree said

with a weary sigh. "I still can't believe what happened."

"I can. I should have anticipated something going wrong." He swung his arm in an arc that encompassed that room and part of the next. "Look at this place. It's no wonder the kids had such a hard time staying out of trouble in here. Anybody would."

"Why? What's wrong with it?"

"Well, for starters, the carpet is practically white. So is the furniture."

"Ecru," Brianne informed him proudly. "The carpet is ivory, and the damask upholstery is ecru."

"Gesundheit."

"Very funny."

"I thought so."

"You would. Well, if you'll excuse me, I have to go get supper started."

"You're cooking? After this morning?"

"Somebody has to." She raised an eyebrow at him. "Unless you're volunteering."

"I boil a mean egg. And I can roast weenies on a stick over a campfire. Does that count?"

"Not for much." She pushed past him and led the way down the hall toward the kitchen. "How did you expect to feed your kids if you can't cook? They'd get pretty sick of peanut butter sandwiches if they had to eat them every day."

"I wasn't worried. Little boys eat anything—except maybe fried liver or Brussels sprouts."

"Oh, what a shame," Bree teased, watching his face so she could enjoy the result. "That's exactly what I was planning to fix for supper tonight."

Chapter Eight

Brianne found a package of chicken strips in the freezer and defrosted them in the microwave. She was fairly well acquainted with the way Emma had arranged the kitchen cupboards and drawers, which helped her function considerably better than Mitch did.

He was so intent on helping her prepare the evening meal he drove her crazy. Finally, after turning around to fetch something and almost crashing into him for the umpteenth time, she decided to banish him.

"Look, I appreciate your efforts. I really do. I'd just rather do this by myself. Okay?"

"Okay. If you insist. Let me get one more thing

and…'' Moving while he spoke, Mitch wound up trying to enter the pantry at the same time Bree was on her way out. They met in the narrow doorway, jostling for room.

Suddenly breathless, she managed to speak, ''Excuse me.''

He chuckled but failed to give ground. ''What's the matter with you? I'd think you'd have figured out by now that I'm not going to hurt you.''

''I know that!''

''Then why do you keep acting scared whenever I get anywhere near you?''

''I'm not scared. You're just in my way, that's all.''

''There must be more to it than that,'' he drawled. ''I think we should stand here like this until you decide to tell me what's really bothering you.''

''Don't be silly. There's nothing to tell.''

Mitch's grin spread, his eyes twinkling with mischief. ''You might as well give in and tell me what's wrong. I've got all day—maybe several. Come to think of it, so do you.''

''Unfortunately.''

He'd placed one hand on the doorjamb on either side of her head. Hoping to escape, she tried to duck under his raised arm.

Mitch was quicker. He caught her neatly and

spun her to face him, holding tight in spite of her halfhearted struggles. "Oh, no, you don't."

"Let go of me. I don't want to play games."

"I'm beginning to think you do," he said.

"Well, you're wrong."

"Am I?" He bent to place a chaste kiss on her forehead, then grasped her shoulders and held her away so he could better study her expression.

"Yes," she insisted.

"Liar."

That accusation took her aback. Was it possible he could be right? Truth to tell, it was getting harder and harder to convince herself she should continue to try to evade him. Worse, he seemed to be reading that fact in her upturned gaze.

Mitch's hold on her shoulders softened. "I'm not a bad guy once you get to know me. I'll admit that having the boys underfoot right now is a drawback, but I can't do anything about that until we're rescued. Then, after things settle down, I'd like to start seeing you."

"Dating me?"

"Yes, dating you. Is that so strange?"

"Actually, yes."

"Why? You don't look like a hermit." He was leaning slightly as if inspecting her. "No long gray beard or anything."

She pulled a face. "I don't get out much, that's

all. I've isolated myself up here because I have to have peace and quiet in order to concentrate on my writing. I'm not much for the social scene. Never have been."

"Well, you have to get away from your computer sometime. Besides, I haven't dated in years. The idea of starting again feels pretty awkward to me, too."

"Really?"

"Really. After Liz left me I considered myself still married so I didn't look for anyone else. Then, when I found out I was getting my boys back, there was so much to do I didn't have time to think about women." The color of his cheeks deepened. "Not much, anyway."

"Why start now?"

Mitch laughed. "I don't know. It doesn't sound like such a bad idea to me. Matter of fact, I'm beginning to like the thought of having someone besides the boys in my life. Maybe you and I were meant to meet like this."

"I sincerely doubt that."

"Why? Don't you believe in divine intervention?"

"Truthfully? I can't say I believe in divine anything. Not anymore."

Softly, he said, "That's a shame. You miss a lot of blessings that way."

"I doubt it."

Certain he was going to back off and let her walk away, Brianne stopped staring into his eyes. That's why she didn't realize he was going to cup her face in his hands until he was cradling her cheeks in his warm, callused palms. At that point, she wouldn't have been able to make herself pull away if someone had yelled that the house was on fire.

Slowly, gently, Mitch tilted her face up as he leaned closer.

Brianne held her breath and waited for his kiss. In her heart she knew it would be wonderful.

She was right. Instead of grabbing her and pressing his mouth hard against hers the way other men had, he kept himself in check, barely brushing her lips with his before easing away.

Was he trembling? Yes! Her eyes widened, and her lips parted slightly as she studied Mitch's face, searching for answers to questions she was afraid to ask. When he looked at her there was a unique intensity to his gaze that left her weak-kneed and reeling.

With her emotions fluctuating wildly and every cell of her body attuned to the man who was still gently caressing her face, all Bree could do was stand there and absorb the precious moments. She pictured herself as a desert wanderer, dying of thirst, who had accidentally stumbled upon an oasis that held the sweetest, most refreshing water imaginable. And she wasn't ready to force herself to stop drinking in that sweetness and turn to face the wasteland. Not yet.

Without conscious thought, Bree raised her hand and mirrored Mitch's actions, drawing her fingers over his jaw and feeling the beginnings of the beard that gave the lower portion of his face a shadowy roughness. To her surprise, he clasped her wrist and stopped her.

"Don't," he warned with unusual hoarseness.

Part of Brianne wanted to remind him that their present encounter was his doing, that she was merely the blameless victim of his silly game.

Another part of her, however, was taking the whole incident far more seriously. Judging by the intensity of Mitch's gaze and the way he was holding her wrist so tightly, she wasn't the only one who had sensed that something important was happening between them.

They stared into each other's eyes for long moments until Bree's brain finally provided an observation that was lucid enough—and innocent enough—to give voice to.

"You need a shave," she said simply.

Mitch released her wrist and stepped back, rubbing his cheeks with his palms and appearing relieved. "Apparently so. I've had other things on my mind lately. Know where I can find a sharp razor?"

Her nervousness remained so heightened it was all she could do to stifle the giggles welling up in her throat. "A sharp one? Picky, aren't you?"

"Well, if I'm going to court you, the least you can do is help me make myself presentable."

"What's your hurry? I thought you said you were going to wait until everything was back to normal."

"I don't want to grow a beard in the meantime," Mitch said with his characteristic lopsided smile. "Not that I expect us to be stuck up here long enough for that."

"Heaven forbid!"

He laughed. "I thought you didn't believe that the Lord might have thrown us together."

"It was a figure of speech," she countered, making a grumpy face to add emphasis. "You'll find disposable razors in the cabinet in the guest bathroom. Help yourself."

"Thanks, I will."

He glanced to where the elements of their evening meal waited. "Sure you can handle this okay without me? I'll be glad to stay and help you get organized."

"Being unorganized is one problem I've never had," Bree said proudly. "Why don't you go shave? And while you're at it, see if the boys are okay, too. I'd hate to ignore them and then hear another crash.''

"You and me both." Mitch pointed to the counter. "I left the spices lined up over there on that end. The marinade for the chicken is in the blue bowl by the recipe card. It smells great.''

"Good. Thanks. Bye.''

"I'm going, I'm going," he said, finally making his exit.

Bree sighed. She didn't want to hurt his feelings when all he was trying to do was be helpful, but she knew if he'd continued to hover over her, watching her every move and getting in the way, she'd have had a terrible time concentrating on anything, especially since their surprising kiss.

No kidding! For some reason, being near Mitch Fowler was making Bree feel more and more like a radio that was only partially tuned in. The signal was there, it just wasn't clear.

Which reminded her. Serenity had its own radio station. She could probably get some idea of what was going on in the immediate area by listening to it.

Encouraged, Bree flicked on the portable radio. A newscaster was speaking. "Flooding is widespread, especially in Fulton, Izard and Sharp counties. Disaster teams are being pushed to the limit. According to state records, the Strawberry River is at its highest level in forty years. Scattered showers are expected to continue through tomorrow. And in the daily farm report, corn futures for October are up a tenth, soybeans are…''

Brianne let her mind drift. Considering all the terrible things that had been happening in the lowlands, she felt ashamed that she'd been so hard on her houseguests. After all, Mitch couldn't help being stranded any more than she could. And his kids probably weren't acting any differently than most children would if they were cooped up in a strange house.

Bree continued to measure spices and stir them into the marinade for the chicken strips. Her thoughts centered on Mitch. She could still see him supporting the weight of her china cabinet, his arm muscles bulging with superhuman effort.

Though she hadn't been conscious of it at the time, she was able to relive the awesome feeling of warmth and power that had radiated from him as she'd helped him right the cabinet. And she remembered with chagrin how she'd berated him afterward. She wished she hadn't been quite so cranky.

Staring at the measuring spoon in her hand, she had to laugh at herself. She could apparently remember minute details of every moment spent with Mitch Fowler, yet she wasn't sure whether she'd added the two teaspoons of red pepper flakes the recipe called for.

The bowl of dark, thick marinade didn't seem to have any flakes in it. Besides, now that she thought about it, it would probably be best to limit the hot spices for the sake of the children.

Brianne measured half the recommended amount of pepper, stirred it into the liquid, then submerged the chicken breasts and put them in the refrigerator. There. That wasn't so hard. As her mother had always said, anyone who could read well could cook well.

Bree studied the rest of the recipe card. Interpretation of Emma's handwritten directions seemed to be the hardest part of the process. Nowhere did the instructions say what to do with the meat after it had been soaked in the spices. If Bree hadn't remembered that her housekeeper had recently prepared the dish, she wouldn't have had a clue that the chicken was supposed to be baked.

Pleased with her progress so far and feeling quite confident, Brianne paused for a relaxing cup of herb tea and straightened up the mess she'd made in the kitchen while the meat marinated.

Then she took out a Pyrex baking dish and carefully arranged the chicken pieces in the bottom. They looked drier than she remembered, so she poured the extra marinade over them before covering the dish with aluminum foil and slipping it into the double oven. Later, she'd bake some potatoes in the second oven.

Smiling, she took off the makeshift apron she'd donned at the outset of her foray into cooking. If this was all there was to feeding a big family, she certainly didn't know what all the fuss was about.

Chapter Nine

By dinnertime, the aroma permeating the house was so wonderful she didn't even have to call her guests to the table. One by one they gravitated toward the kitchen, drawn there by hunger.

Bree tucked a tea towel into her belt to serve as an apron, the way she had before, and greeted them graciously. "The table's all set. Just take your usual places. I'll have everything ready in a jiffy."

"Need any help now?" Mitch asked.

"If you'd get everyone a drink it would be nice," she told him. "Ice water for me, please."

"Coming up."

"I want soda!" Ryan whined. "I always have soda."

Mitch ignored him and set about pouring two

small glasses of milk. Bud was silent. He looked as if he was going to burst into tears when his father put a glass of milk by his plate.

Busy peeling the foil off the top of the casserole dish, Bree asked, "When you finish there, will you get the baked potatoes, please? They're in the top oven."

"Okay. That sure smells great."

"Thanks. Actually, I changed the recipe a little. I was afraid there'd be too much red pepper in it for the kids so I cut the amount in half."

Holding an empty dish to put the baked potatoes on, Mitch cleared his throat. "Uh, excuse me? Did you say you added more red pepper?"

"No, I added less. Why?"

"Because I told you the marinade was ready when I left the kitchen. You didn't need to add a thing to it."

"What? You did not tell me that!"

"Yes, I did. I distinctly recall pointing out that it was already in the blue bowl."

"Well, sure, but you also said you'd laid out all the spices. What was I supposed to think?"

"I don't know. If you hadn't thrown me out of the kitchen you could have asked me."

"If I hadn't let you into the kitchen in the first place we wouldn't have a problem to ask about. I told you I could make dinner by myself."

"Fine." Disgruntled, Mitch turned toward the oven to retrieve the potatoes. When he opened the door, a cloud of steam and smoke billowed out. "What the…"

"What did you do?" Bree demanded.

"Me? Nothing." He waved the fumes away with his hand and began lifting the remains of the potatoes with an oven mitt. "I'll bet you didn't prick the skins before you baked these."

"How was I supposed to know to do that? There's nothing in Emma's files about baking potatoes."

"That's probably because it's so elementary." Mitch stared at her. "Haven't you ever cooked anything before?"

"Not like this. And not lately, except for tonight."

"I wanna send out for pizza," Ryan hollered.

His father was not in the mood to fight with him, too. "That's enough. We can't send out for pizza because we don't have a phone that works—thanks to you and your dog. And the road is washed away so the delivery guy couldn't get it here, anyway."

"I'm not gonna eat that," the boy insisted, pointing at the remains of the potatoes. "It looks gross!"

"Oh, I don't know," Mitch said. "I kind of like exploding food, as long as it's done blowing up before I try to eat it."

Bree was not amused. ''You don't have to rub it in.'' She studied the oddly shaped remnants of skin and fluffy white potato. ''They look kind of like they're double baked, only a lot rougher around the edges.''

''They do, don't they? Wonder if they'd be good with cheese melted on top?'' Mitch put the dish aside and went to the refrigerator to look for a wedge of Cheddar.

Brianne stood back, watching. At the mere mention of melted cheese the younger boy had brightened up. She could tell that Ryan, too, was happy about the cheese idea, though he tried not to show approval. Well, fine. She wasn't trying to starve the poor kids. If they didn't want to eat her potatoes without doctoring them, that was okay with her.

While the cheese and milk were heating in the microwave to make a quick sauce, Mitch got busy scraping the marinade off portions of chicken and cutting them into bite-size pieces for the boys. He cautioned them to wait politely until everyone had been seated before beginning to eat.

Brianne brought a hot dish of canned corn to the table and took her place. Having all of them together at the small kitchen table made things crowded but doable. After what had happened at breakfast she certainly didn't intend to serve the children in the formal dining room and spend all her time worrying about drips on the rug. And she could hardly throw them outside again, since the rain had resumed.

As soon as Mitch returned with the cheese sauce and sat down, Bree took the first bite of her chicken. The initial taste was delicious. By the time several seconds had passed, however, her tongue started to prickle.

That was just the beginning. In less than ten heartbeats the roof of her mouth was on fire. When she breathed, her sinuses felt like she was inhaling pure flame and being seared from the inside out.

Eyes tearing, she grabbed her glass of water and gulped it dry, looking at Mitch just in time to see him sample his entrée. He raised one eyebrow and saluted her with his fork, evidently surprised that it tasted so good.

By the time Bree said, "Don't!" it was too late. His face reddened, his dark eyes widened and his nostrils flared.

Bree couldn't tell if his expression was one of shock, aggravation, panic—or none of the above, since he'd covered his mouth with his napkin and was snorting like a walrus with a bad cold.

One thing was certain. Even though Mitch had scraped the extra marinade off the chicken he'd cut up for the children, they mustn't be permitted to taste it.

Brianne moved to snatch their plates an instant before Mitch did. That set up a clamor from the hungry boys reminiscent of a henhouse being raided by a ravenous fox.

Ignoring the ruckus, Bree and Mitch made a mad dash for the sink and began gulping down cold water. She glanced at him, expecting a tirade. To her surprise, he looked amused.

"I—I'm sorry," she blurted, chancing a smile.

Mitch drew another glassful of water. "No problem."

There was something about the mischievous twinkle in his watering eyes and the twitch at the corners of his mouth that made her giggle. That was all it took to set him off.

He began to roar. Brianne joined him. They chuckled and snickered and laughed and hooted until both were gasping for air.

Tears rolled down Bree's cheeks. She drew a shuddering breath and said, "Oops," which started Mitch off again, nearly doubling him up.

Finally, he managed to regain his self-control. Laying a hand on Brianne's shoulder, he said, "Maybe you'd better retire from cooking while we're still on our feet."

"The exploding potatoes were a nice touch," she countered, bringing more chuckles.

Together, they looked at the table. Both boys

were sitting there, unmoving, holding their empty forks in their small fists and staring at the adults with bewildered expressions.

"Maybe we'd better get clean plates for their potatoes," Bree said, reaching into the cupboard. "Will that be enough supper? All they had for lunch was peanut butter and jelly sandwiches."

"It'll be fine. Put gobs of cheese on his food and any kid will be satisfied," he said. "They could live on the stuff. That, and peanut butter."

Bree winked at Mitch. "Peanut butter on baked potatoes? Yuck."

"Hey," he said, "if I had the choice of another helping of your special chicken or a peanut butter flavored spud, I wouldn't have any trouble choosing."

"You'd pick the potato?"

"Oh, yeah." He nodded solemnly. "No contest."

Mitch had his children bathed and in bed by nine. Ryan was the only one who had argued, and even he had started to doze off almost immediately.

As soon as Mitch was sure they were both sleeping soundly he went downstairs. He'd convinced himself that he was merely looking for something with which to make a list of the items he'd need to replace or repair.

Pen and paper he found easily. When he continued to wander through the downstairs rooms, he was forced to admit he also wanted to see Brianne.

Noticing a light in the library, he headed in that direction. Bookshelves blanketed three walls. On the fourth, French doors opened onto the covered terrace where Bree had taken the children when they'd been caught in the rain while playing outside.

Could that really have been less than twenty-four hours ago? Mitch marveled. How time flew when you were having fun!

The heavy library door was ajar. He cautiously gave it a push, and it glided open effortlessly, quietly. Mitch smiled as Brianne looked up. "Hi. Mind if I join you?"

"No. Not at all."

She was seated on one end of a leather sofa, her feet bare, one leg tucked partially beneath her. She closed the book she'd been reading and laid it aside, then leaned out to peer past him. "Are you alone?"

"Yes. Even Barney's sleeping, thank goodness."

As Bree watched the tall man saunter across the room, she got goose bumps wondering if he was going to join her on the couch. When he chose to sit in a chair, she wasn't sure whether to be relieved or disappointed. Given the choice, she opted for disappointed.

Mitch leaned back, stretched his legs out in front of him with his ankles crossed and sighed. "Boy, what a day this has been. I'm beat."

"I know what you mean."

"So, what were you reading? A cookbook?"

"Very funny. Actually, I don't own a cookbook—which was part of my problem tonight. This book is a mystery." Come to think of it, so is cooking, she thought.

"Ah. Is that the kind of book you write?" he asked.

"Not exactly. My stories are mostly romantic, although I do occasionally work in an element of suspense."

"Love stories? You write love stories?"

"You don't have to sound so shocked."

"I didn't mean anything by it," Mitch assured her. "I'm sure the folks who write science fiction haven't been to outer space, either." The moment the words were out of his mouth he regretted them. "I mean… I didn't mean…" He began to mutter to himself and shake his head.

"I'm not that naive, Mr. Fowler."

"I'm sure you're not." Flustered, he realized he'd insulted her again.

The absurd look on his face made Bree laugh. "I think you're bumfuzzled."

"I'm what?"

"It's one of Emma's favorite expressions. Near as I can tell, it means something between frazzled and confused."

"Sounds about right. Think I should go out and come in again so we can start this conversation over?"

"That won't be necessary." She eyed the paper in his hand. "What are you doing?"

"Making a list. I want you to tell me exactly what was broken."

"Why?"

"Because I intend to replace the busted pieces." His face reddened slightly. "And I'll probably have to buy you a new bathroom door, too, thanks to Barney. He's scratched the inside pretty badly."

"I've been afraid to look."

"Don't. It's not a pretty sight. You'll be glad to hear that the rest of the room is okay, though. Apparently, the only thing he likes to chew is telephones."

"I suppose I should be thankful."

"I sure am." Mitch paused, pen poised, waiting for her to answer his original question. "Well? Which dishes were broken?"

Hearing the fine French china referred to as *dishes* amused Bree. "You don't want to know."

"Yes, I do. I'm serious about this."

"Okay. Let me put it this way. A few years ago,

hand-painted Limoges plates were selling for well over five hundred dollars.''

"Each?"

"Each. And that's if you can find any for sale that match the original set. Of course, the ones signed by the artist can go for double that amount."

"Oh, boy."

"I told you, you didn't want to know."

"You're right," Mitch said, shaking his head. "No wonder you were so concerned. Looks like my son's going to be working off that bill until he's fifty or sixty years old."

"I don't think that's really fair."

"I have to teach him responsibility."

"Within reason," she countered.

Mitch smiled. "Why are you defending him? I thought you didn't like kids."

"I don't."

"You may think you don't. But I've seen you dealing with my boys, and you certainly don't hate them. The dog, maybe, but not the kids."

"Even the stupid dog was starting to grow on me—until he ate the cell phone antenna," she admitted with a wry smile.

"Then liking the children can't be far behind."

"Why? Because they're little animals, too?"

That brought his full-bodied laugh. "You do have an odd way of looking at things, lady."

''I've been told that before.''

''I imagine you have.'' Staring at her, he sobered. ''Have I ever told you how beautiful you are?''

''No.'' It was barely a whisper.

''Then I'm a fool. And to prove it for sure, I'm going to come over there and kiss you again.''

Brianne knew she should tell him not to. She also knew that if she put off doing anything for a few seconds there would be no need. It would be too late. What was the matter with her? Where was her common sense? She was beginning to think and act just like one of the lovesick heroines in her novels.

She closed her eyes. What would she do if she were writing this scene instead of living it? That was the easiest question she'd asked herself in a long time. The first thing she'd do was go back to the beginning of the story and make sure there were no children in the picture. Marriage was hard enough without adding the complications of offspring. She ought to know. She'd overheard her father and mother scream at each other often enough about having a daughter they didn't want. The memory made her suddenly feel queasy.

''Mitch.'' She opened her eyes. ''We need to talk.''

He sat next to her, whispered, ''Later,'' and gently stroked her long, golden hair.

Their lips were almost touching, his breath warm on her face. Trembling, Bree waited. The feather-light kiss she was expecting came, followed without pause by a heavier, more insistent pressure.

Her heart leaped, danced, raced. It was as if Mitch had breached her soul through that simple contact. She wrapped her arms around his neck, meeting him with an eagerness that rivaled his.

Being so near to him left her breathless, and when he pulled her even closer, she wondered if the world had suddenly tipped off its normal axis. *Her* world certainly had! It didn't seem to matter what kind of touch, what kind of kiss, Mitch be-stowed upon her. Everything he did was so astound-ing, so amazingly perfect, she could hardly believe she wasn't dreaming.

Lost in the moment, Brianne was surprised and flustered when he broke contact and set her away from him without warning. This wasn't the way a perfect love scene was supposed to turn out!

She blinked to clear her vision. Mitch was stand-ing there, staring at her as if he'd never seen her before.

"I'd better go," he said, his voice raw with emo-tion.

"Why?"

"Because it's getting late."

The lame excuse hurt so much she couldn't bring herself to argue. "I suppose you're right."

"See you in the morning, then?"

"I'll try to have breakfast ready around eight, if that's not too late."

Frustrated, tense, Mitch combed his fingers through his hair. "Eight is fine. After we get the kids fed I think I'll go ahead and hike down the dirt road a ways, like I said before. Maybe I can see enough to tell how bad the damage is. It's possible a four-by-four could get us out of here if anybody knew we were stranded."

Are you in that much of a hurry to leave? she wondered. She refused to swallow her pride and ask. Instead, she said, "That's a good idea. I keep checking the telephone. The line is still dead."

"Too bad we messed up your cell phone."

A lot of things are too bad, Bree mused. Like the fact that we'll have nothing in common, nothing to hold us together once this calamity is over.

Mitch was edging toward the library door. Brianne wanted to reach out to him, to beg him to take her in his arms, to kiss her again. Instead, she remained quiet and let him go.

She'd known him for what—two days at the most? Yet she was yearning for him like a silly teen with her first crush. That wasn't sensible. Nor was it normal. At least not for her.

Slowly shaking her head, she sighed. It might not make any sense, but it was a fact. She was so enamored of Mitch Fowler, constant thoughts of him were driving her crazy. It had been bad enough before he'd kissed her. Now that he had, she wondered how she was going to cope, how she was going to resist making a blithering fool of herself around him.

A vivid image popped into Bree's mind and immediately struck her funny. She saw herself clad in a long, flowing white gown. Beautifully hued ribbons were streaming from her hair, and she was leaping through a field of wildflowers in slow motion like a ballerina, eventually throwing herself headlong into Mitch's strong, open arms.

The exaggerated spectacle reminded her of the reunion of long-lost lovers in an old movie—combined with a recent TV commercial for the latest allergy medicine!

"May cause unwelcome side effects," she quoted. "And may be habit forming!" No kidding.

There was no use arguing with herself about that. She was already having to deal with plenty of unwelcome side effects when Mitch was nearby, like fluttering heartbeats, sweaty palms and an inability to form sane thoughts. The only good thing about being so dithered was that those strong feelings would eventually help her write better love scenes.

As for the idea that she'd already gotten in the habit of having Mitch underfoot, could that possibly have happened in such a short time?

The answer was a resounding, disconcerting yes.

Chapter Ten

Brianne had never been one to stand by and let circumstances run her life. This time was no exception. When she finally gave up and went to bed that night, she'd narrowed her choices of action to two that were workable.

The way she saw it, she could either try to keep Mitch and his family with her long enough for their initial attraction to wear off, or she could hurry his departure and save herself the heartache she was afraid would eventually come once he realized how incompatible they were.

A soft sound in the hallway outside her bedroom caught her attention. She strained to listen. She couldn't tell if she was hearing a child's sniffling or if Barney had escaped and was nosing around. Either way, the situation called for investigation.

She pulled a light cotton robe over her gown, went to her door and eased it open. Bud was standing there, barefoot, clad in a T-shirt that was miles too big, hugging his bear and wearing the most pitiful expression she'd ever seen.

Brianne smiled and instinctively dropped to her knees so they'd be at the same eye level. "Hi, honey. What's the matter? Couldn't you sleep?"

He shook his tousled head, his lower lip quivering.

Maybe his silence was due to her lack of rapport with small children, but as far as Bree could recall, the little boy had never talked much in her presence. Considering the trauma he'd been through recently, it wasn't surprising he was shy.

Unsure how to comfort him, she decided to start with the obvious. "Are you hungry?"

Again, he shook his head.

"Then what's the matter? Can you tell me?"

Tears began to fill Bud's limpid eyes, making them seem larger and more expressive than ever.

The little boy looked so small, so lost, Bree couldn't resist reaching out to him.

The moment she opened her arms, Bud dropped his teddy bear and threw himself at her, clinging as if he were adrift at sea and she held the only lifeline. His little arms went around her neck and clasped tightly as he buried his face against her shoulder.

"Oh, baby," she crooned. "It's okay. Don't be scared. I've got you. I've got you."

Limitless love poured from her soul and bathed them both in its grace. Brianne couldn't believe what was happening. There wasn't a maternal bone in her body, so what was she doing on her knees in the middle of the night, hugging a frightened, lonely little boy? This experience with the Fowlers was certainly getting complicated.

She began to rock in place, soothing Bud with softly uttered sounds while she mulled over the kinds of support she'd already decided to offer. Helping Ryan would be easy. All she had to do was arrange for tutoring to bring him up to grade level. And Mitch would benefit from her generosity in regard to his lost cabin and personal possessions, so he was taken care of. The question was, what in the world could she hope to do for Bud?

The unspoken answer filled her heart and mind. You're doing it. Just love him.

I can't love him, Bree argued. I can't. It's not in me. I don't understand children. I never have. Look at the way I was brought up. I'd ruin any kid I tried to raise. I know I would.

Tears misted Bree's vision as she held the needy

six-year-old close and kissed the top of his tousled head. This was all wrong! She had her future sensibly planned. It wasn't supposed to include any children.

Maybe I can buy Bud a bicycle or something, she reasoned.

Immediately, her conscience twitched uncomfortably. Shame on you. This is not about money, this is about love.

How could she argue? Apparently, she'd needed a visual aid to convince her this kind of love was possible, because there was no mistaking what was going on. The proof was clinging to her with complete trust and unqualified affection.

"Oh, dear." Brianne started to sniffle the way the child had when he'd first come to her. "Oh, dear, oh, dear."

That was enough to get Bud's attention. He loosened his hold on her neck, then bent to pick up his teddy bear.

He held it out. "Here," he said, clearly yet softly. "He'll make it all better."

She had to fight to keep from weeping out loud. This tenderhearted child, whom she hardly knew, was offering to share his most precious possession. There was no way she'd refuse such a kindness.

"Thank you, honey." Smiling through her tears,

she included the worn teddy bear in their mutual hug. "I feel better already."

"Told ya."

"You sure did."

Still cradling the raggedy toy, she got to her feet and held out her hand to Bud. "What do you say you and I go downstairs and see if we can find some cookies?"

"Okay. Only my bear doesn't like cookies. I'll have to eat his for him."

Brianne laughed and played along. "You're the expert. Shall we bring some back for your brother, too?"

"Naw," Bud said. "He doesn't like cookies, either." His grin spread wide.

"Are you sure about that?"

"Uh-huh."

"Then I guess you'll have to eat his, too, right?"

The little boy muffled a high-pitched giggle with his free hand before he answered, "Yup. I guess I will."

Mitch was already frying bacon when Brianne wandered into the kitchen the following morning.

She yawned. "Do you always get up this early?"

"I like mornings."

"Me, too," she muttered, heading for the coffeepot, "as long as they start around nine or ten."

He laughed. "That's almost noon to me."

"Fine. Then skip breakfast and start with lunch." Another yawn was followed by a sigh. "I told you I'd start cooking around eight, and you said that was fine. If you wanted to eat earlier you should have said so. What time is it, anyway?"

"Around six-thirty." Her resulting groan brought a chuckle from him. "If you wouldn't spend half the night raiding the cookie jar, maybe you wouldn't be so tired."

Her head snapped around so fast she sloshed her coffee. "How do you know about that?"

"My first clue? The crumbs I found in my bed," Mitch said. "Bud crawled in with me sometime during the night and brought a fistful of extra cookies with him. When I asked him about it, he said you and he had been having a late-night snack."

"Us and the bear. So, you didn't actually see us?"

"No. Why?"

"No particular reason. I just wondered." Until she was able to sort out her confusing sentiments she didn't want to get into a discussion about the merits of motherhood versus a life without offspring. And she certainly didn't want to influence Mitch by playing up her newly discovered affinity for one of his children.

She carried her cup to the table and plopped

down. "If I'd realized how early it was I wouldn't have gotten dressed. I'm glad you've decided to cook. I'm beat."

"You look like it," he teased, taking in her light-weight jeans and shirt appreciatively. The blue color almost matched her eyes.

Bree made a face. "Thanks a heap."

"It might help if you combed your hair."

"I did. Didn't I?" She started to smooth her long hair back from her face with her fingers, realized he was right and frowned. "Oops. Guess I forgot. I told you I was tired."

"Don't worry about it. You look kind of cute all mussed like that. It's a good thing you're not trying to cook our breakfast, though. It was interesting enough when you were making dinner wide awake."

"I'd have done fine if you hadn't tried to help."

"The potatoes were good."

"Sure, thanks to your pouring cheese all over them. I told you I didn't know anything about what kids liked."

"You did okay with the cookies last night."

Brianne took a careful sip of her coffee, stalling while she tried to think of another snappy come-back. Before she could come up with one, Ryan dashed into the kitchen, slid to a stop and confronted her.

"Where's the bear?" he hollered. "What'd you do with it?"

Taken aback by his hostility, Bree stared at him. "What?"

"My brother's bear. Where is it? I want it back. Now!"

To her relief, Mitch placed a hand on the boy's shoulder and said, "Knock it off, Ryan. That's no way to talk to Ms. Bailey."

"But—"

"I said, knock it off." Mitch looked to Brianne. "Do you know what he's talking about?"

"Sure. Bud loaned me his bear, that's all. It's fine. I tried to give it back to him last night, but he wouldn't take it."

Ryan stiffened. "You didn't lose it?"

"Of course not. It's right upstairs in my room."

Twisting out of his father's hold, the eight-year-old dashed from the kitchen without further comment.

Puzzled, Bree focused on Mitch. "Okay. You understand kids. What just happened here?"

"Beats me. I've had a hiatus from parenting, remember?"

"At least you were a little boy once. I never was."

"I must confess, I already had that much figured out."

The look Bree gave him in response was so comical he almost burst out laughing.

"What's so funny, mister?"

"You are. I think one of us ought to follow Ryan and make sure he doesn't get into anything that's none of his business. I shouldn't leave the bacon right now. Do you mind doing it?"

"Not at all." Rising, Brianne smoothed her tangled hair. "I have to go upstairs, anyway, and make myself more presentable. The new chef we hired has complained that I'm unfit to grace his kitchen."

"Don't misquote me. I said you were cute that way."

"Cute is for puppies and kittens and little kids. I'd rather look like I have it together, thank you."

"Whatever." With a nonchalant shrug, Mitch turned his back to her and appeared to give the sizzling bacon his full attention. Much of his mind, however, was busy trying to figure out why Brianne seemed unwilling to accept a sincere compliment because she wasn't precisely groomed. Didn't she know how endearing she was when she relaxed and stopped trying to prove whatever it was she was trying to prove?

Then again, maybe it was normal for a woman to think she had to have every hair in place. Personally, he didn't care whether Bree was dressed up or running around the house barefoot. All he wanted to do was look at her, be with her. She was doing everything she could to discourage him, yet he couldn't get her out of his mind for even a few minutes. No wonder he understood kids so well. He was acting like a child. The one thing he'd been told he couldn't possibly have was the one he wanted most.

Brianne met Ryan coming out of her room. "I see you found Bud's bear."

"Yeah."

"I told you it was okay."

His icy glare was unnerving. She refused to be cowed. "Would you like to tell me why you were so worried?"

"No."

"Then how about telling me something about the bear? Where did Bud get it?"

"From our mother. Why?"

"I just wondered."

"It's none of your business," the boy muttered. He tucked the toy under his arm and disappeared down the hall before she could think of a suitable reply.

Astonished, Bree returned to the kitchen.

"Did he find it?" Mitch asked.

"Yes."

"Then why are you frowning?"

"Kids," she said. "I don't understand them at all."

"Welcome to the club. What happened up there?"

"Ryan is furious with me."

"Why?"

"I don't know. He acted like he thought I'd stolen the bear from Bud. It was weird."

"No kidding?" Mitch took the hot frying pan off the burner so he could give Brianne his full attention. "What, exactly, did you say to him?"

"Nothing much. I just asked where Bud got the bear."

"And?"

"That was all. Ryan said it came from their mother."

"You're positive he was mad at you?"

Bree arched her eyebrows. "Oh, yeah. Does his reaction make any sense to you?"

"Maybe." Mitch nodded slowly, thoughtfully. "Ryan hasn't told me much about the years he spent with his mother. I do know he was left in charge of Bud a lot of the time. Maybe he got to thinking of his brother as his personal responsibility. Even so, that's no reason to be rude to you. I'll have a talk with him."

"Forget it. I'm already on his bad side. If he

thinks I ratted on him, he'll be positive I'm one of the bad guys.''

Mitch gave her a lopsided smile. "Guess he doesn't know about the cookie spree you and Bud went on last night, huh?"

"I guess not. Sorry about the crumbs in your bed. I told Bud he could take some cookies upstairs with him. I didn't realize that I should have explained he wasn't supposed to sleep with them."

"Kids take things literally," Mitch said. "If you leave out details, they'll assume there are no restrictions. I'm just thankful you didn't give him something messier."

"Like ice cream." She laughed softly. "He asked for some of that, too."

"Which reminds me. We need to check our food supplies and make sure we ration the important stuff. Just in case."

She didn't even want to consider the possibility of long-term isolation. "I've already looked through the pantry and the freezer. Surely we won't be stuck here long enough to run out of food."

"I'll know more after I've hiked down the road a ways and scoped it out. I want to take a list with me so I'll know what extras to pick up in case I make it as far as Burnham's store."

"Where's that? I've never heard of it."

"It's a couple of ridges to the west of here. When

I was a kid, I used to run errands over that way for my aunt. I hope the old place is still there.'' He smiled in fond remembrance. ''Chances are she didn't need the stuff from Burnham's nearly as much as she needed to get me out of the cabin—and out of her hair.''

''You mean you weren't a lovable little boy like Bud?''

''No. I was more like Ryan—or rather, he's like me. Had a chip on my shoulder the size of a full-grown oak. And just as hard. If it hadn't been for Uncle Eldon taking me in and straightening me out, starting when I was thirteen, I'd probably have wound up in serious trouble.''

''That's too bad.''

''No, it isn't. It gives me insight into what makes Ryan tick. Right now, he's angry at everybody and everything. Plus, he's disappointed in adults. I can relate to that.''

Bree smiled slightly. ''I'm with you so far. When I was little I remember wishing that the neighbors were my parents.''

''At least you had somebody. My folks decided having a kid around was too much trouble, so they tossed me out on my ear.''

''That may have been a blessing in disguise. Your uncle sounds like he was a wonderful influence.''

"He was. Vi and Eldon both were. I intended to teach my kids the same lessons by bringing them out here to the woods. That plan hasn't worked real well so far."

"Don't worry. You'll be compensated fairly for your cabin."

Mitch was slowly shaking his head. "Money's not my biggest problem right now. I was fooling myself to think things would be the same up here now as they used to be. It wasn't just living out in the woods that made the difference in me, it was my aunt's and uncle's kindness, their faith and unconditional love."

"I have faith in you, too," Bree said. "You'll be able to win back your boys once they get used to you again. Remember, three years is a long time."

"Yeah." Mitch sobered. "In their case it's practically a whole lifetime."

Breakfast went off without a hitch. Later, Bree was sitting in the den, reading and watching the boys enjoy morning cartoons, when Mitch joined them.

"Kitchen's all cleaned up," he said. "If I hurry I can be down the hill and back before the kids get hungry again."

Bree smiled at him. "We should be okay till tonight. I found a couple packages of hot dogs in the freezer. I'm positive I can manage to boil a pot of water to cook them in."

"You sure?"

"Absolutely."

"I wish you could come with me." He glanced at the children for emphasis.

Bree understood. "I don't see how. I'll be fine here. I haven't had a good excuse to watch cartoons since I was a kid."

Ryan's attention was diverted. He gave his father a stormy look. "Why do we have to stay with her?"

"Because." Mitch met the boy's animosity with a stern look of his own. "Remember. No running in the house, no noisy games and absolutely no Barney while I'm gone. I want you to behave yourselves just like you would if I was right here."

"Yeah, sure." The sullen child went back to watching television.

Bree followed Mitch from the den and didn't comment until they were out of earshot. "Has he always been so belligerent?"

"No. The Ryan I remember used to be a lot easier to get along with."

"Well, I wouldn't be too hard on him. I imagine his mother told him all kinds of bad things about you to justify her leaving. Being back with you must be a difficult adjustment for him, especially after so long.''

''I hope that's all that's wrong,'' Mitch said. ''If he's scared, I'll cut him some slack. On the other hand, if he's just being a brat, I can't let him get away with it.''

''I'm glad it's your problem, not mine.''

Mitch heaved a noisy sigh. ''Yeah. I've got a lot to keep praying about, all right.''

''For your sake, I hope it helps,'' she said solemnly.

''Always does.''

''Does it? The first night you stayed here, Ryan told me his mother thought you were crazy to believe in God.''

''And you agree with her.''

''I didn't say that.''

''No, but you were thinking it.'' Mitch smiled benevolently. ''Funny how it all worked out in my case. In the beginning, any faith I had came from living out here with Vi and Eldon. They lugged me to their homey little country church when I was so hostile they practically had to hog-tie me to get me in the door. It's a wonder the whole congregation didn't line up to paddle me. I deserved it.''

''What *did* they do?''

''Treated me like a decent human being, mostly. That was a whole new experience for me.'' He shrugged. "Then again, everything up here in the Ozarks was new to me. I'd never seen a live deer before. Or a rabbit, or a nesting bird, or a wild terrapin, or a turkey, or…"

Brianne cut in. "Or ticks, or chiggers, or copperheads and water moccasins, or hail the size of baseballs, or rainstorms that would make old Noah so nervous he'd start building another ark. I still can't believe what happened to your cabin. I'm so, so sorry."

"Don't be. Picturing what might have happened to us if we hadn't made a run for it has put the whole incident into perspective. The old place was in pretty bad shape, anyway. When the boys get a little older, maybe we'll rebuild it together."

"That would be nice. Go on about your aunt and uncle. How long did it take you to quit resisting going with them on Sunday mornings?"

"Sunday mornings?" Mitch laughed. "It was Sunday morning and Sunday night, Wednesday evenings, volunteer work parties for senior citizens and widows, extra Bible study after I finished my school homework and chores, dinner-on-the-ground once a month or more, pie suppers to raise funds for all kinds of charity projects, gospel sings, revivals in a brush arbor—one thing after another. If it hadn't been for doings at church they wouldn't have had any social life at all."

"Where did you fit into it all?"

"It took about four years for them to win me over. I was sixteen when all of a sudden the whole thing made sense to me. I hotfooted it up that aisle so fast one morning when the preacher gave the invitation, I think I scared him silly."

"Do you still go to the same little church?"

Mitch shook his head slowly. "No. It's long gone. Until my family fell apart, I hadn't been in any church for years."

"And then?"

"Then I had nowhere else to turn. I fell back on my raising, as they say. My belief in God and Christ is stronger now than it ever was. Until this week I hadn't missed a Sunday in church for a long time."

"I'm happy for you," Bree said wistfully. "I wish I could say the same. I went to Sunday school when I was little. It didn't stick. When my mother died, so did my faith."

"Lots of people question their beliefs after a trauma. If you aren't in the habit of looking to the Lord for help and trusting Him to work things out, it's easy to go the other way. That doesn't mean you can't choose to turn yourself around."

"And stir up all those terrible feelings again? No, thanks."

"I guess it is easier to stay mad at God."

"I never said that."

"Am I wrong?"

"Dead wrong," she insisted, her jaw set with determination. "Listen. My father went to church all the time, and he was one of the meanest men I've ever known. I have no desire to be around people like that, thank you."

"I'm sorry you feel that way. Just be sure you're not confusing church membership with genuine commitment to Christ. They're not necessarily the same thing. Anybody can warm a pew on Sunday morning without actually belonging. It's like a woodstove with no fire in it. It's still a stove. It looks the same. It can even be stuffed full of firewood and kindling. It just won't function the way it was meant to until you put a lighted match to it."

"Any spiritual fire I ever had is long gone," Bree said.

Mitch smiled knowingly. "That's because no flame will continue to burn unless it's well tended. If you don't want to go back to church, at least consider picking up the Bible once in a while. You might be surprised."

That was what she was afraid of. The disconcerting turn of their conversation had left her unsettled and jittery. As a child, she'd expected messages from God to be delivered to her the same way they had been in biblical times. Angels were supposed to swoop down. Or a finger was supposed to write on the wall. Or bright lights and flames were supposed to miraculously appear and speak.

It was beginning to occur to Brianne that an important part of her psyche may have failed to mature after her mother's death. If that were true, then it was also possible that Mitch Fowler had been sent to awaken her dormant faith.

The whole idea gave her goose bumps. If she accepted that premise, then she'd also have to accept the existence of a God who cared, who watched over His own.

That concept brought her thoughts full circle and slammed them hard against the brick wall she'd built around her heart. If there was a God, He hadn't cared enough to save her mother, so how could she ever hope to trust Him again?

Mitch had been studying Brianne's changing expression as they'd walked and talked. Clearly, she was too overwrought to look after his rambunctious children. Mitch knew Ryan. He'd sense her unsettled state and capitalize on it the minute he got the chance, which would only make matters worse. That left Mitch with only two options. He could either stay at the house with the others or take them all along. He chose the latter.

"Look," he said, lightly touching Bree's arm to get her attention. "Why don't you go dig out those boots you said you had, and we'll all take a hike down the road? The kids need to get out of the house, and so do you. How about it? I promise we won't be gone too long.''

The look in his eyes was so kind it brought a lump to her throat. Seeking to distract herself, to keep from taking him too seriously, she made a joke. ''You sure you're not trying to get me out into the woods so you can ditch me?''

Mitch chuckled. ''If I was going to ditch anybody it would be good old Barney.''

''Now you're talking,'' she said with a silly grin. ''Okay. You go break the news to the kids, and I'll put on my boots. Meet you back here in five minutes.''

Starting away, she paused to add, ''And I like your other idea, too. Don't forget to bring the dog!''

Chapter Eleven

Mitch led. Sullen Ryan was second. Bud was hanging on to his bear for dear life and Bree was plodding along in her heavy hiking boots, bringing up the rear. Only Barney seemed totally thrilled with their outing. He raced in circles, his tiny feet barely touching the ground.

Reaching the end of the driveway where the dirt road began, Mitch paused to let them close ranks, turned and smiled. "Okay. Ready?"

Though Bree knew he'd been asking if they were ready to hike along the damaged road, she couldn't help relating the question to her personal life. Was she ready for Mitch Fowler? For what she might find if she gave herself permission to fall in love with him? Moreover, was she ready to throw away all her previously sensible decisions about her future for his sake and the sake of his children?

Not yet, she insisted, hurrying to keep pace with his longer strides. Not yet.

Soon? her rebellious subconscious asked.

All Brianne could truthfully promise herself was, maybe. That would have to suffice. Under the present trying circumstances, she figured she was doing well to think reasonably, let alone try to adhere to the inflexible ideals she'd set for her prospective mate.

Inside, she was laughing at herself. There wasn't a thing about Mitch Fowler that even remotely qualified him to become her husband. He was the last—the very last—man she should be attracted to.

Yet he was the first who had ever gotten this close to capturing her heart and soul.

Progress was slow because of the children. There was so much mud sticking to the bottoms and outer edges of Bud's sneakers he had to lift his knees in a march step to even walk.

Ryan did better only because he continually stamped his feet. That threw globs of mud against anything within three or four feet of him, including his legs, but at least he was able to keep up with his father.

Bree was not only as encumbered as poor Bud,

she had more trouble keeping her balance than he did. She was toying with the idea of taking him with her and turning back when she noticed with a start that Mitch and Ryan were no longer visible.

"Where'd your daddy go?" she asked the younger boy.

"Over there."

Arms held out for balance, she drew up next to him. "Where? Show me."

He pointed. "I think they fell down."

"Oh, no. Surely not."

That suggestion was enough to flip Bree's stomach into her throat and send her heart on a runaway ride. Grasping the child's hand, she hurried him along. Up ahead the road seemed to vanish. Until they reached that place, there was no way to tell if the drop-off was dangerous.

To her relief, the distance to the bottom of the gully was barely fifteen feet, with a gentle slope. It looked, however, as slick as any plastic slide at a water park.

Mitch smiled from the bottom and held out his hand when he saw her peering over the edge. "Come on. It's easy."

"No way. It's too slippery."

"Don't worry. I'll catch you. If Ryan and Barney and I can do it, you can."

"What about Bud? I can't just leave him up here."

"You're right. Send him down first, then come yourself."

She crouched next to the little boy, sensing his fright. "I guess we're going to have to do this, or Ryan and your daddy will think we're chicken."

A shake of his head was his only comment.

"I know how you feel," she said softly, "but we don't have much of a choice. How about doing it together? We could hold hands. Then you could help me."

To her relief that logic seemed to help. Bud took her hand again and held tight as she straightened. Together they stepped closer to the edge and took their first tentative steps onto the incline.

Brianne felt her feet begin slip almost immediately. She didn't dare let go of Bud, and with no way to stop their rapid descent she had no choice but to balance as best she could and ski directly into Mitch's open arms.

Waiting at the bottom, Mitch saw what was happening and braced himself. If he bent to catch his little boy, Brianne was liable to flatten them both. If he caught her, maybe that would be good enough. He had only an instant to decide.

Bree careened squarely into his chest.

He let out a muffled oof as he seized and steadied

her, hands spanning her waist. A satisfied smile lit his face when he felt Bud's arms grabbing his leg. "Gotcha! Both!"

Ryan was jumping up and down like a cheerleader and whooping with glee. "Good one, Dad!"

"Thanks." Mitch's grin widened. Holding his ground, he used the opportunity to gaze into Bree's wide eyes. "What happened? I thought you guys were coming down one at a time?"

"I needed Bud to help me be brave enough," she said. "I couldn't have done it without him."

"Ah, I see."

"You can let go of me now." Bree pushed the man away, stepped back and nervously ran her hands over her hips as if her jeans needed smoothing. "I shouldn't have let you bully me into trying to do that. My boots didn't help at all."

"Nothing does in slimy clay. Your biggest problem was fear. You were way too tense."

A disclaimer was definitely called for. "Who wouldn't be tense sliding down a mountain of mud?" She tentatively lifted one foot. "Look what it's done to my poor boots! They didn't have a mark on them when we left home this morning. The awful stains will never come out of this suede."

"Good. Then there won't be any reason for you to avoid walking in the woods in the future. You need to listen to the birds, appreciate the wonders all around you, instead of always worrying about everything being perfect.''

Frowning, Bree was still examining her feet. "Perfect? Look at the globs of gunk stuck to my soles. If I walk much farther it'll be so thick I'll be six feet tall, like Bud.''

Mitch chuckled and reached down to ruffle his youngest son's hair as he untangled him from around his lower leg and carefully set him apart, bear and all. "No, you won't. It'll fall off before then. Look. Most of the mud came off Bud when he skied down the hill with you.''

"Nifty. Maybe I should climb up and come down again.''

"Don't do that on my account,'' Mitch quipped. "Catching you when you're going fifty miles an hour is hard on me.''

"Poor baby.''

"I knew you'd be concerned. If you want, we can wait a minute while you wipe your feet.''

"With what?''

"You weren't kidding about being raised in the city, were you?'' he said, grinning. "Since you won't find a boot scraper out here, I suggest you use a clump of leaves or a rock.''

If Mitch had dreamed she'd start to wade into the highest grass along the edge of the road to take his advice he'd have been a lot more specific.

"Not in there!" He grabbed her arm and yanked her clear, careful to keep from flinging her into the boys. "You'll get covered with seed ticks."

"Well, make up your mind." To her consternation, he'd crouched at her feet and was closely examining the denim covering her lower legs. She was about to order him to stop when he mumbled, "Uh-oh. Too late." He began swatting at her ankle.

That didn't set well with Bree. "What do you think you're doing?"

"Saving you from weeks of itching," Mitch said. "If these little bugs have a chance to climb higher you'll be real sorry, believe me."

Bree bent over and stared. "I don't see a thing."

"Well, I do."

"Don't be ridiculous."

"Okay. If you don't want my help…"

She paused long enough to consider his evident sincerity. "Show me one, and I'll believe you."

"I thought Missouri was the *show me* state. This is Arkansas."

"Humor me."

Mitch pinched the fabric near her ankle and held up his index finger. "There. See?"

"No." Bree squinted and peered at his fingertip.

"You're looking for something too big. Think tiny. Almost invisible. Just look for movement—

and hurry up. I don't want this one to decide it likes the taste of me better than it does you.''

Curiosity got the best of Ryan, and he crept closer to see, too. ''Oh, wow! Awesome, Dad.''

Thunderstruck, Brianne realized Mitch had been telling the truth. ''Oh, for…'' Instantly itchy from head to toe she started stamping her feet. ''Ah! Get them off me!''

''That's what I've been trying to do,'' he said. ''Hold still. Stop wiggling around.''

''I feel like they're…'' Glancing at the children and beginning to blush, she broke off and began hitting herself higher on both legs, hoping to do some good. ''Never mind. Just get the rest of them off. Quick!''

Mitch took another couple of hard swipes at the fabric around her ankles, then straightened. ''When you get back to the house you'll need to use bleach on your legs while you shower. That should take care of any I've missed.''

''What do you mean, missed? You can't miss any. They'll bite me!''

''Unfortunately. You shouldn't have waded into that long grass. Big clumps of newly hatched ticks hang on the tips of the tallest blades waiting for a victim to pass by and knock them off. That's why I pulled you out of there so fast.''

"I wish you'd warned me not to get near the grass in the first place."

"I didn't realize I needed to." His grin widened as he vigorously dusted off his hands. "Even the kids know better than to do. that. You mentioned ticks a while back, so I figured you knew, too."

"I do—now," Bree said with a grimace. "Can we go home soon?"

"Gladly. We're almost to where the paved road starts. I'm pretty sure that'll be intact. The bad spots the radio reported should be between here and there. We'll know in a couple more minutes. Think you're up to finishing the hike?"

Brianne didn't answer except to break away while he was still speaking and begin clomping down the middle of the rutted road. Gummy clay coated the soles of her ankle-high boots and rolled up along the sides, hampering her progress. She persisted until the worst of the accumulation had sloughed off, glob by glob.

"Hey. Slow down and wait for the kids." Mitch's longer strides brought him even with her. "This isn't a race."

"It is for me. The sooner I get out of these clothes, the better I'll like it." Cheeks flaming, she cast him a sidelong glance then lowered her voice so the boys couldn't overhear. "Don't look so smug, mister. You know what I meant."

"I'm not smug," Mitch argued. "I know exactly how you feel." It was his turn to blush. "And you know what I meant."

Brianne couldn't help smiling. "Maybe we'd better quit talking before we're both any more embarrassed." She paused, listening. "Is that a motor I hear?"

"I think so!" Mitch looked back and motioned to the plodding boys. "Come on, you guys! We hear a car!"

The road ahead was narrow and winding with a few drop-offs. It was those places that showed the worst damage, the deepest cuts. Small valleys made the sound of the engine echo, confusing the direction it was coming from. All Mitch could hope for was that the vehicle they'd heard was on the same trail they were.

Bree lagged. "Slow down. You're killing us."

"You don't want whoever it is to get away, do you?"

"Of course not. Maybe you should go on ahead. I'll bring the kids. None of us are used to running in pudding."

"Feels more like cold oatmeal to me," Mitch countered. "You know. Gummy."

"What a disgusting thought. I don't think I'll

ever eat oatmeal again without thinking of this. Yuck.''

''I didn't like the stuff in the first place,'' he said. ''Give me ham and eggs any day.''

''Stop. You're making me hungry again.''

''That's because you didn't eat enough of the great breakfast I cooked. You don't know what you missed. Barney loved the leftovers.''

''Brag, brag, brag. You're insufferable.''

''Thanks.''

They rounded a corner masked by a thick stand of oaks and came upon the source of the noise. A white pickup truck with a county logo on the door sat on the opposite side of a wide fissure. The driver was gunning the motor. A second man was leaning on the handle of a shovel and squinting at the mired rear of the truck.

Mitch waved and shouted at them across the mucky chasm. ''Hey! Over here!''

The man with the shovel spat into the dirt and slowly made his way around the truck to join his partner. As soon as the driver shut off the truck's engine, the man cupped his hand and called, ''You folks all right?''

''As all right as a person can be when he's stranded,'' Mitch shouted. ''How soon before you guys fix this road?''

The driver climbed out and waved. "That you, Mitch?"

"Yeah. Charlie?"

"In the flesh. What're you doin' up here?" With a chuckle he added, "Never mind. I can see what you're doin'."

Embarrassed, Brianne sidled away from Mitch and folded her arms while she watched the children approach.

"It's not what it looks like," Mitch said. "My car's stuck in a ditch up on Nine Mile Ridge. Any chance you can send somebody up there to pull it out for me?"

"'Fraid not. That road's messed up worse'n this one. We should have this place fixed in a day or so, though. Gotta get some good fill dirt in here and tamp it down. If we don't have any more gully washers it won't take long."

"What do you know about the phones?"

"Not a thing. That's not our department," Charlie said. "We've got enough problems with these here roads. You wouldn't believe the mess that storm made."

Mitch frowned. "Oh, yes, I would. Remind me to tell you about it when I get to town."

"Hey, I see you got your boys," the other man said. "They okay, too?"

"Fine. We're all fine. Right now we're staying at the Bailey place."

"Don't recall anybody by that name up this way," Charlie said. "Do you, Sam?"

The other man shook his head. "Nope. Must be newcomers."

Brianne stepped forward and tapped Mitch on the shoulder. "I have an unlisted number. Give it to them in case the phones start working, and then let's get back to the house. I itch all over."

"Okay." He shouted the numbers across the void as she recited them to him.

"Got it," Charlie said. "Take care a yourself, Mitch. I'll do what I can." Pausing, he glanced at the rear of his truck and snorted in disgust. "As soon as Sam gets me dug out, that is."

Mitch waved goodbye and turned to go, finding Bree and his sons thirty feet ahead of him, and headed the way they'd come. He hurried to catch up.

"Wait for me."

Busy trying to keep her balance on the uneven, slippery road, Bree barely acknowledged him until he pulled even with her and asked, "What's your hurry?"

She gave him a dirty look. "I think I feel ticks in places I didn't even know I had."

"Well, don't take it out on me. It's not my fault

you were too prissy to put up with a little mud on your shoes."

Ryan's resulting giggle put her in an even worse mood. "Prissy? Ha! I'm not having trouble putting up with anything but you," she declared.

Although Mitch didn't reply, his hurt expression made her conscience twitch uncomfortably. What was wrong with her? Why was she being so unkind to him all of a sudden? When you got down to basics, their present situation wasn't really his fault any more than it was hers.

Bree slowed and held out a hand to him. "I'm sorry. I shouldn't have snapped at you. I guess I'm just frustrated about this whole thing."

"That makes two of us," he grumbled.

"I know. I said I was sorry." The hint of a smile lifted one corner of her mouth.

"What's so funny?"

"I was just thinking." The smile grew. "I've finally found something you and I have in common. We're both in a really bad mood today."

Chapter Twelve

Mitch didn't talk any more than necessary as they struggled home via a roundabout course. His thoughts, however, were loud and clear. It didn't matter how attracted he was to Bree if she refused to give herself permission to consider him, or his family, as anything other than a nuisance.

There had been a few times since they'd met when he'd imagined an equal interest on her part, but she'd always managed to counter his enthusiasm with a big dose of reality. Lots of people survived an unhappy childhood to go on and lead a normal life, yet she was apparently determined to cling to the past. The question was, why?

Why, indeed. Beneath Bree's capable, self-confident facade he'd sensed the heart of a lonely, lost little girl. It was as if she was afraid to let anyone know she cared. Or was afraid to let herself become emotionally involved in the first place. The way she was acting right now, chances of his ever finding out which were slim and none.

They crested the final hill to arrive at the broad, sweeping lawn surrounding her house. Grass along the outer edges had grown noticeably after the heavy rain. Bree picked her way carefully past the tallest clumps.

Mitch had been carrying Bud most of the way home. He set the boy on his feet next to Ryan to wait for Barney while he reassured Bree. "You're probably safe from ticks this close to the house. Whoever mows the lawn has kept it short. That discourages bugs."

"Oh, goody. I'm so glad to hear my gardener is doing it right." She was out of breath and once again sounded curt.

The perplexing conversation he'd been carrying on within himself had left him irritable. His primary urge was to grab her, hold her tight, and kiss her senseless in spite of her off-putting attitude. Taking that course of action was probably the worst thing he could do, especially in front of the boys.

Then again, Mitch wasn't feeling very smart or very rational. He was physically weary and emotionally on edge. Only one thing seemed certain.

Soon, the road would be opened and he'd have no excuse to be near Bree. If she refused to see him socially, as he suspected she would, he'd never get the chance to show her how right they could be for each other.

Looking at his impulse in that light gave it more credence. He hurried to catch up with her before she reached the rear door.

"Wait!"

Startled by the urgency in his voice, she hesitated and looked back. "Why? What's wrong?"

"I forgot to give you something."

Before she could ask what, he'd reached out, pulled her into his arms and kissed her with such intensity that she felt weightless, senseless—wonderful!

Conscious thought fled, replaced instantly by intuitive response. Brianne closed her eyes, clung to him and returned his kisses with all the pent-up fervor she'd tried so hard to hide from everyone, including herself.

This isn't love, she kept insisting. It's just a normal physical reaction to being kissed so passionately.

The only problem with that premise was that she was positive she wouldn't feel the same way if any other man were delivering those gentle yet demanding kisses.

Head spinning, Brianne fought to resist the insistence of her heart that Mitch Fowler was special. It was no use. She'd lost the fight before it began. There was only one thing to do—surrender, melt into his arms and return his kiss with all her heart and soul.

She'd almost forgotten they weren't alone when Ryan's high-pitched voice intruded on her bliss. He squealed, "Eeew. Gross!"

That was jarring enough to cause Bree to break off their mutual kiss. She turned her head, pressed her palms to Mitch's chest and tried to push him away. To her surprise he held her tight. The restriction only intensified her desire for freedom.

"Mitch, no." There was muted alarm in her tone. "We can't let this go any further. Remember the children."

He frowned, stared into her eyes. "Further? I wasn't trying to seduce you, Brianne. I wouldn't treat you that way even if the kids weren't here. I care for you. Why can't you see that?"

She didn't know how to respond. Possible seduction hadn't been a conscious part of her thoughts until he'd mentioned it. Now that he had, however, the disturbing notion refused to go away. Had he been telling her he cared merely as a prelude to a physical relationship? Maybe. That was the way her manipulative father had always approached her mother after one of their terrible arguments.

The comparison made her shiver. A few seconds ago she'd been every bit as vulnerable as her mother used to be. Doubt surfaced. "Why me?"

By this time, Mitch was at the end of his tolerance. He'd given it his best shot when he'd kissed her. If she couldn't accept or understand the feelings he had for her, there was no use beating her over the head with them.

"Because I'm nuts," he said dryly.

Brianne realized immediately that she had destroyed what had remained of their romantic mood. Somehow, her pride carried on, substituting tongue-in-cheek humor for the ache in her heart. "I could have told you that."

"I'm sure you could have." Mitch not only stepped back, he shoved his hands into his pockets to keep himself from reaching out to her and shot her a look of annoyance. "Well, I suppose we might as well go in the house."

"I suppose so."

Exasperated, he looked at his eldest son. "You. Take off everything that's muddy and leave it outside on the porch. Then march straight to the bathroom and get into the shower."

"Bud, too?"

"Bud, too. And Barney," Mitch said flatly.

"You're all taking a bath. You might as well do it together."

The boy pouted. Looking from his father to Brianne and back, he muttered to himself.

"One more word out of you and you'll spend the rest of your life locked up with that dog," Mitch threatened. He realized immediately how petulant and childish the warning sounded, but at the moment he didn't care one whit.

"I wish we'd never come here," Ryan countered, glaring at Brianne.

Mitch didn't hesitate. "Yeah. Me, too."

Well, Brianne noted, the Fowlers were beginning to sound more and more like a normal family. Not that that was a positive change. The look in Ryan's eyes had made the hair on the back of her neck prickle. His animosity couldn't have been clearer if he'd been shouting curses at her through a megaphone.

Bree was curled up on the sofa in the den, reading and absently scratching a red spot on her ankle, when Mitch found her later. She'd donned shorts and a sleeveless shirt so her clothing wouldn't irritate the bites she'd gotten on their hike.

One eyebrow rose as he noticed what she was doing. "Don't scratch that. You'll make it worse."

"Considering how badly I itch, I suppose I owe

you a big thanks for knocking most of the bugs off,'' she said.

"You're welcome.''

He was looking at his feet instead of at her. Bree thought he seemed unduly nervous. "Did you want to talk to me?''

"Yes. About what happened this afternoon—I'm sorry. I know I was wrong.''

Wrong to kiss me? Or wrong to get so mad at Ryan when he interrupted us? she wondered. "I'm glad you came and found me. I've been wanting to talk to you about Ryan.''

"What's he done this time?''

"Nothing. It's just that he still seems awfully angry with me. Is it normal for kids to hold a grudge like that?''

"I don't know. I remember feeling unsettled at his age, but that was because my parents kept telling me I'd ruined their lives. In spite of Liz's poor choices I know she loved the boys. And so do I.''

"Have you told them?''

"Sure,'' Mitch said.

"In so many words?''

"Words can be overrated.''

"I suppose they can. So, what's the deal with Bud's teddy bear? Do you think it's some kind of security symbol for him and Ryan? Like a tangible form of reassurance?''

Mitch combed his fingers through his hair. "Beats me. If I didn't think taking that toy away would cause more trouble than it's worth, I'd get rid of it in a heartbeat. I'm just worried that Bud would fall apart if I did. I guess I'll have to wait till he outgrows his fixation."

"Oh, sure. I can picture him going off to college with that old bear hidden in his suitcase," she said, smiling. "Especially if Ryan has anything to do with it. Do you think it would help if you came right out and asked Ryan why he's so miffed at me?"

"Does it matter?" Hopeful, Mitch paused, studying her expression.

Brianne shrugged. "A few days ago I would have told you it didn't. That's changed. I can't explain why, it just has."

"Could it be that you *like* my kids?"

"Of course I like them. Sort of. They can't help it that they're young and totally confusing to me, any more than I can help feeling lost when I try to relate to them. For kids, I suppose they're not half bad."

Mitch's smile spread into a grin. "Thanks."

"You're welcome. So, will you have a talk with Ryan for me, after all?"

"Sure. Do you want to listen in?"

"No! That's the last thing he needs. He's already

sure I'm the enemy. If you make it look like you've sided with me, you'll destroy any progress you may have made toward winning his trust. At least I think you will, assuming there's any logic to kids' thoughts.''

"We can hope." Mitch reached for the doorknob, then hesitated. "What about the rest? You know."

"I do?"

"Yes."

She could swear he was blushing, which meant he was probably referring to their kiss. And what a kiss it had been!

"I don't know what you're talking about," Bree said.

"Liar."

"There you go again, besmirching my character."

"At least I'm consistent," Mitch countered.

"About some things."

Mitch started to leave, then paused again. "Oh, I meant to tell you. Dinner was great."

"Thanks." She laughed softly. "If I'd managed to ruin hot dogs and canned baked beans I'd never have lived it down. Oh, well, at least the kids liked it."

"And nothing exploded," Mitch quipped. "I would have complimented you at the time, but the boys were making so much noise all I wanted to do was get them fed and out of the kitchen.''

''No kidding! I can see why people with children put picnic tables in their yards. They can't stand the constant mayhem inside the house.''

''We should be gone in a couple more days,'' he said. ''Think you can keep your sanity that long?''

''I'll try.''

In the back of Bree's mind was the certainty that the Fowler children weren't *half* the threat to her well-balanced life—or to her sanity—that their father was.

She picked up her book again but found concentration difficult, so she laid it aside and turned her thoughts to her unfinished manuscript.

Silently critiquing her characters, she realized she'd have to go back and make some changes, thanks to the time she'd spent around Mitch. Although he was far too human to be considered a role model for a hero, he had awakened her to a part of her subliminal self that had been a surprise. Obviously, she'd had a warped view of the way men's minds worked. Then again, there was no guarantee she understood Mitch's motivations any better than she did those of her fictional heroes!

The urge to go turn on her computer was great. She wandered to her office and decided to chance it. There hadn't been any noticeable power fluctuations for a long time, and she backed up everything she wrote on floppy disks anyway. If, heaven forbid, her computer did get toasted by an errant jolt of electricity, it wouldn't destroy her work to date.

Bree was seated at her desk, absently staring at the monitor and waiting for the necessary programs to load, when Mitch interrupted. "May we come in?" Ryan was with him.

"Of course. I just sat down. I'm not working yet."

"Good. Ryan has something to say to you."

The boy scuffed his bare toes against the carpet and made a face as he stared at the floor. It wasn't until Mitch nudged him that he looked up and spoke. "I...I'm sorry, Miss Bailey."

Bree smiled and pushed back her swivel chair. "Apology accepted. How about some cookies?"

"No, thank you," Ryan said soberly. "I'm not allowed to have any more."

"Oh? Why not?"

"'Cause I busted your dishes."

Looking from the boy to his father, she arched an eyebrow.

Mitch was shaking his head. "There's a lot more to it than that. I've been trying to explain the difference between being truly sorry and only pre-

tending to be in order to get rewards. I think my
rationale got lost in the translation when I mentioned eating your cookies in the same breath with
holding a grudge.''

"Probably," she said with a light laugh. "All
this talk about cookies has made me hungry,
though. Suppose we go see how many are left in
the jar and divvy them up evenly. That way, you
and I can eat a few now, and the boys will be sure
we've saved some for them. Then they'll have
something to look forward to when you're ready to
let them have another treat.''

To Bree's surprise, Ryan didn't argue. He looked
at his father and didn't say a word.

"You can go," Mitch told him. "It's almost your
bedtime, anyway. Carry Barney out the back door
and let him go potty, then put him in the bathroom.
When you've done that, maybe you and Bud can
have one cookie and a little glass of milk.''

"Yes, sir.''

Impressed, Brianne stood with Mitch and
watched the eight-year-old walk slowly down the
hall, his bare feet padding on the dark tile. "I think
you're making progress," she said softly.

"It does seem like it." In a show of frustration,
Mitch raked his fingers through his hair. "Trouble
is, I won't know for sure if I've done things right
until he's grown up, and then it'll be too late.''

"He'll be fine. They both will be."

"I'm not as worried about Bud," Mitch said. "He's a different kind of kid."

"He's also younger, more impressionable," she reminded him. "Surely that makes a difference, too."

"I suppose so. What they both need is a decent mother—someone like you."

Bree held up both hands as if fending off a literal advance. "Whoa. Stop right there. You said it all when you said a decent mother. Their first one wasn't exactly mother of the year. Don't make the same mistake again."

"Meaning?"

"Meaning, I decided a long time ago that I was never going to subject any child to the kind of upbringing I had. Period. Relationships are too tenuous, too apt to fall apart. Putting kids into the mix only makes things worse."

"Or better," Mitch countered.

"Don't count on it. People tend to repeat the same mistakes they were raised with, whether they mean to or not. That's a statistical fact. I don't intend to saddle myself with such a serious responsibility."

"You don't believe in the healing power of love? How can you write the kind of books you do if you don't buy into the illusion?"

"Illusion is the right word," Bree said. "Just because I can create a believable fantasy on paper doesn't mean I think I can do it in real life."

Mitch took a step closer, then stopped when he saw her tense up. "I think you could," he said quietly, "if you weren't afraid to try."

Chapter Thirteen

Bree would have left him standing there and re-treated into her office behind closed doors if she hadn't been afraid that doing so would affirm his erroneous opinion. Instead, she put on a pleasant expression and led the way to the kitchen.

Bustling around, she set the cookie jar on the table and reached for the can of coffee. "Shall I make us a cup?"

"Only if you have decaf," Mitch said wearily. "I haven't been sleeping well. More caffeine won't help."

"Okay. Decaf it is." She went to work measuring as she continued their conversation. "You'll sleep better when you get your own roof over your head again. I wish I'd been able to find you a permanent place before your stupid dog ate my phone.''

He sank into a chair at the table, his shoulders slumping, his elbows propped in front of him, fingers laced together. ''If you'd bothered to ask me in the first place, I'd have told you I had a place in town. As a matter of fact, I remember trying to tell you at least once.''

''When?''

''I don't know.''

''Roughly?''

''I think it may have been about the time you'd run down the battery in your cell phone. You were so overwrought you wouldn't listen to a thing I said.''

''Well, you could have kept trying,'' Bree said, annoyed. ''I've been worrying myself sick about where you were going to live. Why the sob story about the cabin if you weren't homeless? Were you getting even with me?''

''Of course not.'' Mitch heaved a noisy sigh. ''Do you always think the worst about everybody or do you save that attitude exclusively for me?''

''I'm an equal-opportunity cynic,'' she said. ''Even Ryan had me fooled.''

''About what?''

''The big house. He said you sold it to get the

money to look for him and Bud, and that was why you all had to go live in the old cabin.''

"That's more of his scrambled logic," Mitch countered. "I did have an expensive house. And I did sell it. True, most of the money went into the long-term search for Liz and the kids, but I'm not destitute. I never said I was. Matter of fact, I distinctly remember telling you that I built houses for a living.''

Brianne racked her brain. Had he? Probably. Whenever Mitch was speaking she'd constantly had to fight to keep her mind from wandering the way it did when she was formulating a plot for one of her stories.

"Okay," she admitted, "maybe you did say something about having a job. But that doesn't mean I understood what you meant.''

"Why not?"

"I don't know.''

"I think I do," Mitch told her. "You were judging me by what you could see. You'd decided from the get-go that I was a poor hillbilly without a dime so you didn't pay attention to anything I said that might have changed your mind.''

"I did nothing of the kind!''

"Oh, no? I lived in a cabin with no running water or indoor plumbing. As far as you knew, I was raising my sons there. When we got flooded out, I showed up with a handful of possessions and nothing else.'' He huffed in disgust. ''I'm surprised you even let us in.''

In retrospect, so was she. Normally she'd have been so apprehensive of a knock on her door in the middle of a storm she'd have hesitated to answer it at all. Yet she had. And had immediately taken in the waifs on her doorstep as if she were running some kind of halfway house for soggy ragamuffins.

The analogy brought her up short. That *was* how she'd viewed Mitch and his family, wasn't it? Well, it wasn't her fault. He'd certainly looked the part both times she'd seen him.

''I suppose I should apologize,'' Bree finally said. ''I'm still getting used to living out here in the country. Nothing is like where I came from. It's a whole new world for me.''

''I don't doubt that.''

''You don't have to sound so smug.''

''Yeah, well, I'm sorry, too.'' He picked up a cookie and studied it to give himself something to do besides look at Bree. He finally took a bite and chewed slowly. ''Now that I think about it, I was doing the same kind of thing with regard to you until recently.''

Bree was puzzled. ''You were?''

''Yes. I'd made up my mind that you and I could

never get along together because of this fancy-schmancy house of yours and the way you live.''

"You were right.''

"Nope,'' he drawled. "I was wrong. If you were really as prissy as I'd thought, you'd have thrown us out on our ears long ago.'' He chuckled. "Especially Barney.''

Mitch's good humor was affecting Bree's mood. "That had occurred to me. Often. I'd have done it, too, except I didn't want the kids to pitch a fit.''

"I don't buy that. You've gone to a lot of trouble to try to convince me you don't like the boys. If that were truly the case, you wouldn't care how upset they got.''

"Sure I would. I'm not mean.''

An enigmatic smile lit his countenance. "My point, exactly.''

By the time Bree and Mitch left the kitchen it was after ten. Yawning behind his hand, he bid her a polite good-night and said, "Guess the kids forgot their cookies and went straight up to bed. I'll go tuck them in. See you in the morning.'' He started up the stairs.

"Good night.''

Trapped amid whirling emotions and confused thoughts, Brianne headed toward her office. There was no way she could recapture the mood to work on her book. Not tonight. Not after the disturbing conversation she and Mitch had just had. It didn't matter that he'd been dead wrong about her. Once real life intruded and she lost the feeling that she was a part of her ongoing story, her creativity vanished.

She knew she could either be sensible and quit for the night, or sit at her computer and stare blankly at the blinking cursor while her mind wandered. In other words, the lights were on but there was definitely nobody home.

The door to her office stood ajar. Pushing it all the way open, Brianne froze, puzzled. Something looked wrong. Her desk chair had been rolled up to face the computer, and although she couldn't see anyone sitting in it because its back was toward the door, she could look past it and see colorful figures dancing across the edges of her monitor screen.

She stared, openmouthed and unbelieving. Then, she launched herself across the room with a yowl that could have been heard all the way to Little Rock—and probably was.

"No! Not my computer!"

She grabbed the back of the swivel chair and spun it around. There sat Ryan, hands in the air as if he were an arch criminal who had just been caught red-handed by the police. Bud, who was squeezed into the chair beside him, puckered up to cry.

Apparently Ryan had been balancing the keyboard in his lap, because when Bree moved the chair, the short cable beneath the keyboard held it back and sent it crashing to the floor.

"I don't believe you did this!" she screeched. "How could you? How dare you? You're supposed to be in bed!"

"It's just a game," the older boy said. "We didn't hurt your stupid computer."

"Stupid computer?" Bree howled. "It's my whole life! My business. I can't work without it."

"So?"

"So? So?"

She was so angry at the inconsiderate child she didn't know what to do or say next. Mitch appeared in the doorway just in time. Bud bailed out of the chair and ran to him. Ryan went, too, though he took his time.

Scowling, Mitch looked to Bree for answers. "I heard you screaming all the way upstairs. What happened?"

"I caught them playing with my computer!"

"Did they hurt it?"

What a stupid question. "I don't know. What difference does it make. *Nobody* touches my computer. Nobody!"

"Don't you think you should check it before you come unglued? Kids are pretty savvy about electronic gadgets these days. Chances are, it's fine."

"That's not the point."

"It's exactly the point," Mitch argued, keeping his voice even, his attitude calm. "I'm going to take the boys upstairs and put them to bed now. Then I'll come back down here. While I'm gone, I want you to carefully check your files."

Taking the boys by the hand and turning to go, he paused. "If you expect my children to be drawn and quartered for touching your computer, you're going to have to prove to me that they've actually destroyed it."

Brianne was playing computer solitaire when Mitch returned.

She glanced at him with a disgusted expression. "Everything's fine."

"I thought it would be."

"No, you *hoped* it would be. There's a big difference."

"I'll give you that one," he said, sauntering across the room and perching on the edge of her desk. "If it's any consolation, Ryan says he's sorry."

"So what else is new?"

"Well, at least he's going to get used to apologizing. I'm sure it's a skill he'll need plenty in the years to come."

"Undoubtedly." Abandoning her half-finished game, Bree scooted her chair back. "I hope I scared him good."

"You must have," Mitch said. "You terrified me. I thought for sure there'd been a murder down here or something."

Bree smiled. "There almost was."

"That's what Bud figured. He was a lot more scared than Ryan. It took me a long time to get him calmed down."

"Oh, dear." The smile faded. "I didn't mean to frighten him like that. I just saw what was going on and reacted instinctively. If anything happens to my computer I'm out of business. Did you explain that to the boys?"

Mitch chuckled under his breath. "Sort of. I think I said something about you being crazy and unstable."

"Oh, that's close. Poor little Bud." Rolling her eyes and shaking her head, she stood and headed for the door. "I'm going up there right now and explain it to him."

"Okay," Mitch said, following, "but if he's already asleep I'd appreciate it if you didn't wake him. He's had a pretty rough time the last couple of days."

"He's had it rough? What about me?"

"Okay. None of us have had an easy time of it," he agreed with a weary sigh. "But it'll all be over soon. After we're gone, I hope you'll remember us fondly."

Remember them? She'd couldn't have forgotten the Fowlers if she'd tried. Nevertheless, Bree wasn't about to let herself be drawn into another serious discussion about her personal feelings. No, sir. Especially not when a still, small voice kept insisting that she didn't really want the road to be repaired. Not soon. Maybe not ever.

Logic told her they couldn't continue the way they had been for much longer, though. To begin with, she'd soon run out of food. It was amazing how much the four of them had already consumed, even if you didn't count the meals she'd partially ruined or the leftovers she'd given the dog.

Other staples were in short supply, too. Right after Barney had dined on her cell phone, he'd decided to shred several extra rolls of toilet paper for dessert. Add laundry soap and paper towels to that list, and they'd soon be in dire need.

Climbing the stairs a few steps behind her, Mitch spoke softly, sincerely. "I want you to know, as soon as I get back to town, I'm going to make every effort to let folks know there was nothing funny going on up here."

"Funny? Like what?"

"You know. Hanky-panky."

She giggled. "Do people still use that expression?"

"They do around here. And their moral code dates back to the old days, too. Charlie's bound to mention having seen us together. I don't want anybody saying or thinking anything bad about you on my account."

"That's sweet. But you don't need to worry about my reputation. I've already told you I don't get out much. By the time I've lived here awhile they'll all be sure I'm some kind of nutty recluse, anyway. Which I am."

"That could change." Mitch had closed the distance between them, and his breath ruffled her hair as he spoke.

Barely ahead, Brianne sensed his nearness. Her steps slowed at the top landing.

After what seemed like eons, Mitch finally came closer and wrapped his arms around her. She laid her arms over his and leaned against his strong chest with a sigh.

The quiet hallway wrapped them in the cocoon of its dimness and made Bree feel as if they were the only two people in the world. If only that were so. If only her waking dreams could come true. There was a rightness, a flawlessness in Mitch's touch, in his nearness. It was the rest of their world that was all wrong.

Tears blurred her already cloudy vision. Closing her eyes, she wished she were the kind of person who could pray, believing her plea would be heard, because this was the perfect time to ask God for a miracle.

Mitch bent to place a kiss on her hair, then whispered, "I'm going to miss you, honey."

She couldn't speak, couldn't make herself respond in kind. No matter what she said it would only make matters worse. A solitary tear slid down her cheek and dropped onto his arm before she could catch it.

Once again, he leaned and nuzzled her hair, kissing her ear, her temple, the corner of her eye and finally her cheek. She was crying. For that he blamed himself. He'd pushed her too hard. Too fast. Because he'd managed to fall in love in the space of a few days, he'd made the mistake of believing it could be mutual.

He turned her in his embrace and lifted her chin with one finger so she'd have to look at him. "Ryan isn't the only one who needs to keep apologizing. I'm sorry, Bree. I wasn't trying to torment you. I just didn't want to leave here without telling you how I felt."

Mitch bent to place a chaste kiss on her trembling, moist lips, then straightened and held her away from him. "Do you understand what I'm trying to say?"

Her silent nod was his answer.

"Good. Then I think I'd better leave you now, before I have to lie to your neighbors about what did or didn't go on while I was staying with you." He managed a tenuous smile. "You can talk to the boys in the morning. We'll all feel a lot better in the daylight."

She watched him turn and walk away. Standing alone in the long hallway, she realized she'd never felt more isolated, more bereft, in her entire life.

Feel better in the daylight? Her thoughts echoed. Now that *would* be a miracle.

Chapter Fourteen

The following morning, Brianne accepted Mitch's offer to help her prepare a second meal of pancakes, but only because their food supplies were getting scarce, and she couldn't afford to make another error and waste precious ingredients.

They were both in the kitchen, sidling around and trying to work without getting too close to each other, when they heard a rumble in the distance.

She stopped in the midst of setting the table and turned to him. "Is that thunder?"

"No. I don't think so. It sounds like heavy equipment to me. Maybe Charlie and his crew have started working on that part of the road, like he said they would."

"Oh." Bree felt numb. Time was running out.

Ryan came barreling into the kitchen, almost knocking the plates out of her hands. "Dad! Is the road fixed?"

"If it isn't, it soon will be," Mitch said. He carefully flipped the hotcakes he'd been tending. "Go get your brother and be sure your hands are clean. Breakfast is almost ready."

Ryan left the room the same way he'd entered, at a dead run, shouting, "Bud! We get to go home!"

"How long do you think the repairs will take?" Bree purposely avoided eye contact with Mitch so she wouldn't inadvertently reveal her disappointment.

"There's no way to tell. Hours, days. It'll depend on how much clay is in the soil and whether or not they have to truck in a lot of fill dirt and rocks, I suppose. Why?"

"I just wondered."

"You aren't going to miss us, are you?"

"Of course not!"

"Uh-huh. That's what I thought." Mitch knew he'd sensed a lot more emotion in her denial than she'd intended. Still, as long as she kept refusing to consider the prospect that they might be right for each other, there was nothing he could do or say that would change things between them.

Of course, there was also the possibility that he

was mistaken, Mitch admitted ruefully. He'd consciously placed his whole life in God's hands before he'd gotten his boys back. Nothing had happened since then to change that unwavering commitment. Consequently, it made sense to conclude that if the good Lord had wanted him to stay with Brianne long enough to convince her they were compatible, He wouldn't have let the crew repair the road so quickly.

Mitch huffed in disgust. It was a lot easier to trust the Lord for answers to prayer when he was getting exactly what he'd prayed for, wasn't it? No kidding! It was also easier when he thought he'd figured out just what God's aim was in a particular situation. In this case, he didn't have a clue, unless... Unless he was supposed to be helping Brianne instead of the other way around!

Looking at the present dilemma in that light gave him a broader scope of ideas. As folks said, it isn't over till it's over. Therefore...

"Once the road is passable, would you mind driving us down to Serenity?" Mitch asked.

"What about your car?" She sounded disconcerted. "You can't just abandon it."

"I figured to get a few friends to help me. We can come back later and use my work truck to pull the car out."

"Oh." Bree didn't think her raw emotions could

withstand the stress of a prolonged drive to town with Mitch Fowler seated next to her, yet she saw no graceful way to refuse. "Well, I suppose I can drive you. That is, providing the road is good and solid. I don't want to get my car stuck, too."

He flashed her a winning smile. "If we get stranded we can always hike back up here like we did before."

"No way. I've tromped around in enough mud to last me the rest of my life, thank you."

"Speaking of mud, I noticed that the creek below the spring is running normally again. You don't intend to rebuild your lake, do you?"

"Not a chance," she said quickly. "If I want fresh fish I'll buy it in the market."

"You like to fish?"

"You don't have to sound so surprised. Fishing was fun the few times I tried it. I figured, if I stocked the pond well, it would be a good source of natural food."

Mitch laughed at her naiveté. "Have you ever cleaned a fish?"

"No. So what? How hard can it be?"

"That's not the point," he said, continuing to chuckle. "Trust me. It's *way* too messy for you."

His smart-alecky attitude and the strain of knowing he'd soon be out of her life for good coupled to make her unduly short-tempered. "When are you going to stop assuming I'm some kind of obsessive cleanliness nut? Just because I don't happen to be a slob doesn't mean there's anything wrong with me.''

"You're right,'' he said sagely. "There's not a thing wrong with liking nice things. Or with getting dressed up to go to town occasionally. Take Sunday mornings, for instance. I'll bet you'd feel a lot better about me if I showed up in a suit and tie when I picked you up for church.''

Brianne crinkled her brow, stared at him. "What are you talking about? I never said I was going to church with you.''

"No, but it's safe. And public. And it will certainly help your reputation if you let me introduce you to the folks in town that way.''

"I told you. I'm not worried about my reputation. I don't want to meet a lot of new people. I like my solitude. I need to preserve it in order to work, remember?''

"So you said. What happens when you run out of ideas? Where do you go to recharge your batteries, so to speak?''

He had a point. Though books and movies were good as far as they went, it was more intellectually stimulating to interact with real people. Still, she wasn't keen on going to church with him. There was something awfully personal about it.

"Thanks, but no, thanks," Bree said.

"Are you afraid?"

Her head snapped around, her eyes narrowing. "Of course not. You don't scare me one bit."

"I wasn't talking about me," Mitch said. "I was talking about God."

"That's ridiculous."

"Is it? You told me once that you used to be a believer—until your mother died."

"So? What did I know? I was just a kid."

"When it comes to God, we all are," he argued. "There's nothing wrong with that. It's not a sin to ask questions, either. Or to doubt God's love or His wisdom when we're faced with loss. I did the same thing when my boys disappeared. The sad part is when a person gets stuck in that rut and never works through it."

"I'm not stuck in any rut," Bree said flatly.

A broad grin spread across Mitch's face. "Good. Then as soon as the boys and I are settled in town and the phones start working again, I'll call you and we'll pick a Sunday that's good for both of us."

I won't go, she assured herself. Call all you want. I won't go. I won't go. I won't go.

The return of the exuberant children didn't distract her. Nothing did. All during breakfast and the cleanup afterward the same declaration kept run-

ning through Brianne's mind. She nurtured it as if
it alone would ensure her unwavering resolve.

Adamant, she convinced herself that if she'd had
her computer powered up she'd have programmed
the negative statement into a screen saver!

Ryan was in the yard with Barney, so he was the
first to spot the approach of their rescuers. He bar-
reled into the house with a whoop that almost
scared the poor dog into having another accident.

Everyone headed for the front porch to see what
all the shouting was about. Bree paused just outside
the door while the others ran ahead to meet the
approaching vehicle. It was a medium-size truck
with a light bar mounted above the cab and a second bench seat behind the driver.

Her heart lodged in her throat. She edged closer
to listen to what was being said. Mitch was gestur-
ing to the men in the mud-caked volunteer fire department rescue truck and pointing to the canyon,
telling the story of what had happened to his cabin.

Three men in heavy yellow coats climbed out of
the truck. Mitch shook hands with them, then
looked at his children.

Bree heard him say, "Okay, boys. The firemen
are going to give us a lift into town if we hurry.
You guys need to go back in the house and gather
up your stuff."

Then he looked at Brianne. "Guess you're off the hook. You won't need to drive us home, after all."

"Good." She lifted her chin, managed a slight smile. "Whatever you do, don't forget to take the dog."

Chuckling, Mitch stepped closer and gently grasped her hands. "There are lots of things I won't forget, especially your kindness and tolerance."

"Or the fact that it was my fault you almost got killed."

"Nobody's perfect," he said, caressing her knuckles with his thumbs. "But I will have to admit, you're closer than most."

"Thanks. I think."

"You're welcome." Mitch released her. "Well, I guess I'd better go get my gear, too. Not that there's a lot of it. I just don't want you to have to clean up after us when we're gone."

He hesitated, looking from the house to the waiting fire truck. "Uh-oh. I just thought of something. I won't have time to scrub the spare bathroom before I go."

"That's okay," Bree said. "Now that the road is open, Emma will be coming again soon. Whatever cleaning I don't get done, she can finish."

"Okay. But that bathroom door will have to be

replaced. I'll measure it the next time I'm here, then pick one up and install it for you later."

Bree couldn't stand there and allow him to talk about their nonexistent future for one more second. "That won't be necessary. I'll call the firm that remodeled the house before I moved in and have them handle it. That way, you won't have to bother, and everything will be sure to match."

Sighing in resignation, Mitch nodded. "Okay. Have it your way." Backing away he added dryly, "Perfect, as usual."

Rather than go into the house while Mitch was inside, Brianne waited on the lawn for the little family to come out. When they did, Mitch herded them past her as if she were of no more interest to him than one of her ornamental shrubs.

"Bud and Ryan, you ride in the jump seats," he was saying. "I'll take Barney with me. Let's go. Move it."

Ryan obeyed easily. Bud lagged behind, then doubled back to Brianne. There were tears in his eyes.

Overcome with more affection than she'd thought possible, she dropped to her knees and took his little hand. "You be a good boy, okay?"

Sniffling, he nodded.

Fighting her own tears, she smiled at Bud, gave

him a tender hug, then set him away and kissed his damp cheek. "I love you, honey. You remember that. Okay?"

"O-kay."

"And take good care of your bear."

"Okay." Hesitating, he sniffled again and looked at Brianne, his eyes glistening with more tears. "I want you to be my new mama."

That did it. Bree began to weep silently, unashamed. "Oh, honey, I wish I could be, but life doesn't work like that. Grown-ups have a lot of other problems to worry about. Not everybody in your family likes me the way you do. You wouldn't want them to be unhappy, would you?"

The child burst into tears and threw himself at her, clinging to her neck with fierce determination. She struggled to her feet and carried him to the rescue truck, no more willing to let go of him than he was to release his hold on her.

I won't have Mitch Fowler feeling sorry for me, she lectured herself. I can't let him see how upset I am.

While Mitch was leaning into the truck to check Ryan's seat belt, Bree handed Bud to one of the firefighters and hurried toward the house.

It would have been gracious to stand on the porch, put on a brave front and wave a friendly farewell to her accidental guests. Unfortunately,

Bree knew she didn't have enough self-control left to manage it.

It hurt too much to even *think* about what was happening. Seeing Mitch and the boys driving away would be far more pain than her wounded heart could take.

"Cute dog," the youngest firefighter said. He and Mitch were leaning against the rear of the truck's cab, watching the road play out behind them while the others rode in the seats up front. Barney was curled in Mitch's lap, shivering in spite of the warm day.

"The kids found him during the storm," Mitch said, petting the dog to soothe it—and himself. "I hope nobody comes forward to claim him when I place an ad in the lost and found. We're all pretty attached to him already."

"I can see why. He does look kind of lost. Course, so do…" He stopped talking and looked away.

Mitch knew exactly what he'd left unsaid. "My boys? Yeah, I know. They've had it pretty rough lately."

"I heard Miz Fowler'd died a while back. Sorry about that. So, you and the writer lady fixin' to get together after all a this? You could do worse 'n her, that's a fact. 'Sides, I heard she's rich."

Mitch glared at him as if the other man had just spit in his face. "I suggest you keep your opinions of Ms. Bailey and me to yourself." His voice was almost a growl. "You get my drift?"

"Yes, sir, Mr. Fowler," the younger man said. "Ain't none of my business who you're living with. No, sirree. If you and her want to shack up, nobody's gonna hear about it from me."

Furious, Mitch figured it was a good thing he had to keep holding on to the dog to keep it from jumping out of the moving truck. If he'd had both hands free, he might have done something he'd have been sorry for later.

He clenched his jaw. This was exactly the kind of wild rumor he'd been worried about.

If he'd had only his welfare to consider when he learned that Brianne was living alone, he'd have left her house immediately, before anyone found out he'd even been there. Responsibility for Ryan and Bud, however, had eliminated that option.

Although he hadn't consciously made the choice to damage Brianne Bailey's reputation, he had chosen to put the health and safety of his sons first. It had been the right thing to do. Unfortunately, this was the result.

Denial of any wrongdoing would only sound like an excuse and make matters worse. If Bree didn't get out of that house of hers pretty soon and personally demonstrate the kind of upright, virtuous person she really was, there was no telling how bad the gossip would get.

Maybe she didn't care, as she'd claimed, but *he* did. She'd rescued his family, and he was going to see to it that she didn't have to pay any higher price for her good deed than she already had.

And as for himself? Mitch snorted in disgust. The price he was paying was infinitely higher than a mere reputation. Being around Brianne had cost him his heart and soul. Whether he'd ever be able to reclaim them remained to be seen.

Chapter Fifteen

For days after everyone else had left, Brianne had wandered aimlessly through her cavernous house, unable to concentrate, unable to work. Without Mitch and the boys underfoot, the place seemed more than empty. It seemed desolate.

Everything she saw, everything she touched, reminded her fondly of them—even the cookie crumbs she'd found in the boys' bed when she'd stripped off the sheets and gathered them to be washed.

"I'm hopeless," she murmured. "Absolutely hopeless."

She paused on the upper landing of the staircase, hugging the loose bundle of sheets and remembering the last time she and Mitch had stood there together. Could he have been trying to say what she'd thought he was? Or was she reading more into his declaration than was really there because affection was what always developed in the stories she wrote?

Her sensible nature came to her rescue. There was no way two people could fall in love in just a few days. Those kinds of things only happened in fairy tales. She and Mitch might have felt some fondness for each other due to the stressful situation they'd been trapped in, but that didn't mean they'd found anything lasting. They couldn't have. They hardly knew each other.

The sound of an approaching car caught her attention. Now what?

Bree had missed out on her housekeeper's usual Thursday session because the phone lines hadn't been repaired in time for Bree to call and assure the older woman that the road was safe. By the time she'd finally reached her on Friday night, Emma had insisted she wasn't free again until the following Tuesday. Could she have taken pity on her part-time employer and come early, after all?

Hopeful, Bree listened. The car was slowing. She dropped the loose sheets in a pile on the entry floor and hurriedly threw open the front door.

An unfamiliar pickup truck with an extended cab had stopped in the driveway. A well-dressed man was getting out. It couldn't be! It was. Mitch Fowler!

She gaped in awe. His hair had been trimmed and was neatly combed. A dark blue suit accented his trim frame, making his shoulders seem even broader, his waist more narrow. He was wearing a pale blue dress shirt and silk tie. Bree was flabbergasted. If she'd passed him on the street she might not have recognized him.

Behind him, a small arm was waving to her from the rear seat of the shiny black truck. It looked like Bud. She returned the greeting. "Hi!"

Mitch smiled, eyeing her. "I like that outfit. It looks nice and cool. But I'm afraid shorts aren't really appropriate for where we're going. How long will it take you to change?"

"What are you talking about?"

"It's Sunday. We've come to take you to church."

Bree backed up, hands raised to fend him off. "Oh, no, you don't. You said you'd call first."

"You have an unlisted phone. I couldn't call."

"Hey, that's not my fault. You could have asked me for the number if you'd really wanted it. You were here long enough."

He shrugged, pushed back his cuff to check his watch. "I know. My error. So, you coming with us? The service starts in forty-five minutes."

"No way."

"Okay. But if we backslide it'll be your fault."

Mitch opened the passenger side door of his truck and folded the front seat forward to make it easier for the boys to clamber out.

"Come on, guys. It'll get too hot to sit in there for long. You can run around on the grass while I talk to Ms. Bailey. Just try to keep your new clothes and shoes clean, will you?"

"Yeah!" Ryan shouted. Hitting the ground, he immediately raced for the back of the house with his brother in pursuit. As always, Bud's bear made it a threesome.

Mitch was removing his suit jacket and loosening his tie as Bree asked, "Where's Barney?"

"Home." He gave a short laugh. "I didn't think you'd appreciate riding with him."

"That's a pretty truck. It looks new."

"It is. I wanted something that was roomy and safe for the kids. It had to come with four-wheel drive too, so we wouldn't get stuck again. This seemed to fill the bill." Mitch laid his jacket neatly over the back of the front seat, tossed the tie in after it and slammed the door.

"Can you afford it?"

"Yes. I told you I'm not broke. So, shall we go inside?"

"Well… The place is kind of a mess."

"Never. Not your house."

Brianne pulled a face. "I missed Emma's regular Thursday session last week."

"I'll manage to tolerate the clutter, no matter how bad it is," Mitch teased. He casually looped an arm around her shoulders. "Come on. I need a big dose of that air-conditioning you keep on all the time."

What could she say? All her mental rehearsal had been in vain. He'd already thwarted her by not insisting she drop everything and attend church with him.

"All right. But one joke about lousy housekeeping and out you go."

Laughing heartily, he escorted her to the door. "I wouldn't dream of it. So, tell me…what have you cooked lately?"

Bree was in a perfect position to elbow him in the ribs, and that's exactly what she did. Mitch's resulting *oof* made her giggle. "Hush. You deserved that, and more."

"Probably." He'd released her and was feigning injury by rubbing his ribs. Then he spotted the pile of sheets on the floor and switched to visible shock. "What happened there? Did a laundry truck wreck in your foyer?"

"I warned you…"

"Okay, okay. Let's go into the kitchen so we can

watch the boys from the windows. They may look like they've reformed, but believe me, the change is mostly on the outside.''

"I should have complimented you," Bree drawled, eyeing him surreptitiously as he led the way down the hall. "You cleaned up nicely."

"Told you. It's the suit."

"I meant the boys. They look really nice this morning," she said, suppressing another giggle when Mitch turned to give her a derogatory look.

She crossed to the kitchen sink and peered out the window above it. "Speaking of which, I don't see them."

"Well, they can't have gone far. Not in those shoes. They're brand new. I had to sandpaper the soles to keep them from slipping on the carpet at home."

"Did you get settled in okay? I was worried you might need some help, but I was as cut off as you were. I didn't ask for your address or phone number, either."

"I'm in the book," Mitch said absently. Leaning past her, he began to frown when he couldn't spot his children. "Excuse me a minute. I think I'd better go check on the kids."

It never occurred to Brianne to let him do it alone. Once outside, she had to half run to keep up with his long, purposeful strides.

He called, "Ryan!"

She thought she heard a faint answer from the direction of the canyon where the stream ran.

"Over there," she said, pointing.

Mitch was way ahead of her. Breaking into a run, he sped across the wide lawn, not slowing until he reached the ruptured clay knoll that was all that remained of her manmade dam. He stopped, looked over the edge.

Thirty feet below, Ryan, muddy and crying, was struggling to keep his footing on the slick slope.

Without a moment's hesitation, Mitch plunged over the edge toward the frantic boy.

So did Bree.

Brambles and sharp twigs scratched her bare legs below her shorts. Mud and slimy dead leaves squished into her sandals and between her toes. She ignored the discomfort. All that mattered was reaching Ryan and finding out what was going on.

Mitch got there first. "Where's Bud?"

Shaky sobs kept the eight-year-old from speaking clearly enough to be understood. Frantic, Mitch grabbed him by the shoulders. "Calm down. What happened? Where's your brother?"

"Down there," Ryan said. "The bear fell."

"In the water?" Mitch shouted.

Ryan nodded vigorously. "I—I tried to stop him. I told him I'd get it for him, like always, but—"

Before he'd finished speaking, Bree was on her way again. Wherever Bud ended up, she knew it would have to be lower down the slippery hill. She didn't even want to think about the possibility he might have jumped into the creek to rescue his teddy bear. The water wasn't deep, but it was swift. Dangerous. And still filled with debris from the flood.

Tree branches hung in her path and slapped her face, her bare arms. Saplings bent under the weight of her body as she passed over them, then snapped back like a whip.

She could hear Mitch crashing through the brush, gaining on her, but there was no time to worry about holding the branches to keep them out of his face. Poor little Bud was in danger. Mitch was on his own.

Breathless, she cried, "Bud! Where are you?"

There was no answering shout. Not even a whimper.

Closing in, Mitch echoed her call. His voice was hoarse, breaking with emotion. "Bud! Bud!"

Bree could see the slope easing. Ahead, the creek widened. White water boiled over the remains of a fallen oak. Its broken branches extended like claws, bare of leaves and reaching for the sky in one last, silent plea.

Her heart stopped. Was something small and

brown caught in the undertow beneath the tree's battered trunk? There was only one way to be sure. Grabbing wildly at passing vegetation to slow her descent, Bree threw herself over the bank and into the racing water.

Mitch read purpose in her headlong leap. He slid to a stop, gasping for breath, and flattened himself on the ground on his stomach, one hand holding fast to a snag, the other reaching out over the water toward her. "Brianne! Do you see him?"

Her head broke the roiling surface of the icy water. She coughed, gagged. There was pathos and desperation in her eyes.

"Did you see Bud?" Mitch shouted again.

"No. Just the bear," she answered. "I felt all along the bottom. There's nothing else here."

"You sure?"

"Positive."

Mitch scrambled to his feet, staggered, slipped. Wild-eyed, he stared at the water as it cascaded down the canyon.

"Go!" Bree waved her arms and yelled at him. "Leave me. It's not deep here. I can stand. I'll be all right. Go! Go!"

To her relief, Mitch followed her orders and quickly disappeared past the fallen tree. She made one last underwater foray to satisfy herself that she hadn't overlooked any clues, then pulled herself to the bank, tossed the teddy bear onto higher ground and crawled out after it.

Remaining on her hands and knees for a moment to catch her breath, Bree shivered. It wasn't because she was chilled. It hurt to inhale, to move. Her ribs felt sore, like one of those jagged limbs might have poked them without her realizing it. Maybe it had. So what? That kind of minor injury didn't matter. Not now.

She hauled herself to her feet, pushed her wet hair from her face, then pressed a hand to her aching side, held it tight, and set off to follow Mitch down the canyon.

She couldn't see him because of the thick vegetation, but she could hear him shouting for his missing son. That was enough to keep her going.

The ground started leveling out. The streambed was lined with enormous black rocks that looked like they'd been stacked one atop the other in flat, uneven layers by some giant hand. Over time, running water had polished the exposed surfaces, making walking on the rocks treacherous.

Drawing ragged breaths, Brianne paused to listen. She could still hear Mitch in the distance. What else? Was that a child sobbing? The sound was growing louder. Bud? Anxious, she looked around, hoping, praying.

No, it was Ryan. Her heart plummeted. The older

boy was running blindly along the opposite bank, weeping as he went. He was soaking wet, like her, and muddy from head to foot. Apparently, he'd been in the water, too, and had saved himself. If only Bud were big enough, strong enough, to do the same.

More frantic than ever, Bree kept pace with Ryan by staying on a parallel course. This was a nightmare. It couldn't really be happening. She hadn't felt this helpless, this defeated, this alone, since the night her mother had died.

As always, that memory triggered turbulent, unsettling emotions that filled her mind and heart. Yet this time was different. Bree was able to picture herself, not as a child but as a *parent*.

Suddenly she realized that, unlike her mother, she was capable of loving others enough to put them first, to care about them more than she cared about her needs or wants, to give them the kind of altruistic love she'd been denied as a lonely, frightened little girl. And she owed her awakening to Mitch and his boys.

None of the usual arguments surfaced to dissuade her, to make her question her conclusions. On the contrary, every beat of her heart was further affirmation that she was, indeed, a different person than she had been before she'd met the Fowlers. Before she'd accidentally fallen in love with Mitch.

It was a miracle! And the answer to her long-ago prayers for healing after her mother's untimely death. She owed her heavenly Father more thanks and praise than she'd ever be able to deliver.

Right now, however, she hoped God would understand that she had more pressing concerns. Poor little Bud was lost, maybe fighting for his life.

That thought almost made her cry out. She wanted to fall to her knees in anguish, to beat the ground with her fists and plead with God once again.

Instead, she did what she knew she must. She breathed a simple prayer and kept going. "Father, help us! Please! I'm so sorry I doubted You."

It wasn't very eloquent or very practiced, but it was the best she could do. And it was the most sincere prayer she'd ever prayed.

As if in answer, she heard Mitch shout, "Bud!" at the top of his lungs. The call didn't sound worried or plaintive, like the others had. It was the kind of triumphant cry a father would make if he'd located his missing child.

Chapter Sixteen

Brianne arrived at the muddy, rock-edged pool seconds after Ryan did. Two dark heads were bobbing together in the water. The older boy didn't hesitate. He ignored Bree's screeched command—"Ryan, no!"—and jumped in, feet first.

His splashdown was so close to his father and brother he made a wave that washed over them and temporarily kept Bree from seeing whether or not Bud was all right. It never occurred to her to sit on the creek bank and wait patiently for someone to eventually tell her.

Instead, she followed Ryan's lead, although with a lot less forward momentum.

The current wasn't nearly as swift as it had been in the steep canyon. The water came to her waist, and she waded to Mitch and the boys on leaden legs. Covering those few yards seemed to take an eternity.

Her first indication that all was well was Mitch's whoop of triumph. Holding Bud tight to his chest, he closed his eyes for a moment, then opened them to gaze at the little boy with so much love, Brianne wept for joy.

Ryan had already joined his father and brother in their mutual hug. The instant Bree was close enough, she was included, too.

It was hard for her to tell if the others were laughing or crying. Little wonder. She wasn't sure exactly what she was doing, either. But who cared? All that mattered was that Bud was safe. They were all safe. And well. Her prayers had been answered. God was so good!

Mitch's hearty laugh warmed her in spite of the icy water and the aftereffects of her fatigue. Her answering grin was so wide it made her cheeks hurt—until she decided he might be laughing at *her*.

She paddled her arms back and forth and braced her feet wide on the creek bottom to hold her position while she made a face at him. "Okay, mister. What's so funny?"

"You are. You should see yourself!"

"Well, you're not so spiffy, either," Bree countered with a toss of her head and a swipe at the bangs plastered to her forehead. "At least I started out casually dressed."

"You mean you're not still impressed with my suit and tie? How about the boys? Don't they look nice?"

"Wonderful." Bree's tone was filled with love. She reached out and ruffled Bud's hair and would have done the same to Ryan if he hadn't ducked around his father, out of her reach. "I've never seen them look more adorable."

Softening, she gazed into Mitch's eyes and added, "Their daddy looks pretty good to me, too."

"You sure? We're all awfully dirty."

"I know. I noticed. I don't suppose you guys have a change of clothes with you, do you?"

"Nope."

"That figures."

Mitch was chuckling. "I would have brought extra clothes if I'd known swimming was on today's agenda."

"Never mind trying to make plans," Bree said. "The way your family finds trouble, I think you should start carrying an overnight bag with you all the time. You're bound to need it sooner or later." She grinned. "Probably sooner."

"And maybe a life raft, too?"

"Good idea." Brianne kept listing things for his amusement. "And sunscreen, and packets of food, and bottled water, and lots of towels. Oh, and a leash.''

"For Barney?" Mitch asked.

"No. For Bud's bear." She flashed a smile of encouragement at the soaking wet little boy and told him, "Your bear is fine, honey. I found him up the creek."

"You did?" The child's voice was barely audible.

"She sure did," his father assured him. "I saw her. She jumped right in and rescued him."

"I could of done it," Ryan grumbled.

Brianne was too elated, too relieved, to take his grumpy mood seriously. He was giving her his usual testy, temperamental look, and she wasn't about to let him get away with it. Not this time.

Instead of making unwarranted apologies, she raised her arm and crooned, "Oh, Ryan…''

The minute he turned his head to look at her she smacked the surface of the pool with the heel of her hand and sent a rooster tail of creek water right into his face.

Sputtering, he blew water out of his nose and mouth. His eyes widened in shock, looking bigger and darker than she'd ever seen them. Before he had a chance to recover and complain to his father, Bree splashed him again.

That second affront was all the boy could stand. He drew back his thin arm and retaliated.

Mitch had glanced over to see how Ryan was reacting to Bree's teasing. Unfortunately, the boy was so excited he failed to control his aim. Part of the spray he threw at Bree made it all the way to her face. The rest smacked into his father's head.

Feigning anger, Mitch roared and splashed Ryan. Ryan splashed him back. Bud was caught in the middle and getting well doused from both sides. He began to squeal and flail his arms, flinging droplets in no particular direction.

Bree didn't play favorites. She wildly sloshed as much water as she could at everyone. The advantage was clearly hers because she was the most mobile. Continuing to hold on to Bud gave Mitch only one free hand with which to defend himself, so she started to work her way around to his opposite side, hoping to limit his ability to strike back.

Ryan had ducked behind his father and was holding on to the man's broad shoulders, trying to use Mitch's bulk as a shield.

As soon as Mitch discovered what the boy was doing, he spun around and inundated the contentious eight-year-old. "Oh, no, you don't. Take that!"

"No, Dad, no!" He spit. Blew like a beached whale. "I give. I give!"

"Oh, yeah? We'll see about that."

"But Dad," the boy yelled. "I didn't start it."

"No, you didn't, did you?"

Mitch stopped splashing. Then suddenly, as if obeying a silent command, all three Fowlers turned on Bree.

"Get her," Mitch hollered.

Ryan was all for it. "Yeah! Drown her!"

"No!" Brianne had to keep her hands in front of her face in order to draw enough breath for a screech of protest, which meant she couldn't fight back. When she saw Mitch swing Bud around so the boy could hang on to him piggyback style, she knew it was payback time. Mitch could use both hands. She was really in for it.

He held out his arms and began to paddle water at her so fast it felt like he was dumping bucketfuls over her head. Burying her face in her hands, she squealed and turned away, heading for the nearest bank.

"Oh, no, you don't," he shouted. "Come back here."

"No!" Bree stumbled, lost her balance.

Mitch caught her from behind, closed his strong arms around her waist and lifted her half out of the shallow water. "Gotcha. Now try and get me wet."

"Let go," she begged through her giggles. "I'm

sorry. I didn't mean to splash you. I'll never do it again. Honest.''

"Dunk her, Dad. Dunk her," Ryan urged.

Mitch was chuckling. "How about if I kiss her, instead?"

"No!" the boy said. "Dunk her."

"I will—if she doesn't quit wiggling."

Brianne got the message. Gasping for breath, she stopped trying to pry loose his grip and forced herself to relax. "Okay, okay. I'm not fighting you anymore. See? Truce?"

"It better last," Mitch said. "No funny stuff."

She held up her hands in exaggerated surrender. "I'll behave. I promise."

"Then what are we all standing here for?" Mitch said wryly. "Personally, I'm not crazy about becoming crawdad bait. Let's get out."

By hanging together and helping each other, they managed to reach the bank without too much slipping, sliding and tripping.

Mitch set Bud out of the water easily, then put his hands on Bree's waist and gave her a boost, intending to do the same thing for her.

Unfortunately, the bank was so slick in that particular spot she couldn't get a firm hold. Losing traction, she slid into the pool—and into Mitch's arms—with a splash and a giggle.

"Lift me a couple of inches higher, and I'll make it the next time," she said.

"You could put one foot in my hands and I could throw you up there, too, but I don't recommend it." He set her aside. "Stand right here. I'll climb up and pull you out."

Ryan had already clambered out by himself when his father breached the bank and turned to give Bree a hand, as promised.

As the furor died, Bree realized how totally spent she was. She found a flat, accommodating rock and plunked herself down on it to rest. Judging by the look on Mitch's face when he joined her, he was exhausted, too.

Bud wiggled into the narrow space between them and yawned.

"My sentiments exactly," Bree said. "I sure wish it wasn't uphill all the way to my place."

"Yeah. Me, too. But it really isn't as far as it felt like on the way down."

"Let's hope not." She sighed, stretched her legs in front of her and ran her hands over the damp skin to check for injury. To her delight, none of the scratches were deep. "That was some trip."

"Are you okay?"

"I'll live. I think the cold water actually helped. Before I got wet, my ribs were sore, too."

"We'll probably all be pretty sore tomorrow," Mitch said.

He smiled, leaned closer and put his arm around Bree's shoulders to pull her to him as he glanced at his youngest. Bud had laid his head on her lap and was already half asleep. "Except maybe for him. He wasn't quite as stressed as the rest of us were."

"Which reminds me. We need to pick up his teddy bear on our way home. I think I can remember about where I left it."

Ryan spoke. "Hey, Dad! I lost a shoe. Can I go back in the creek and look for it?"

"No way." Mitch was far too thankful to waste energy getting mad over something that trivial. Instead, he teased, "I thought I told you guys to keep your new clothes clean."

Bree gave a little giggle. "Hey, we can't get much cleaner than we are now."

"I never thought I'd see you involved in a mess like this."

"I learned everything I know about having fun from you and the boys," she told him, flipping her wet hair with a quick toss of her head. "Well, that was exciting. What shall we do next?"

"It'll be pretty hard to top our trip down the canyon. How about we quit for the day?"

"Good idea. What do you say we all go back to

my house, get cleaned up and fix something to eat? I'm suddenly starving.''

Ryan looked askance. "Not me. Not if she's going to cook.''

Mitch laughed. "Tell you what. We'll all cook. I vote we skip the exploding potatoes this time, though. They're too hard to scrape off the oven walls.''

"Picky, picky, picky.'' Bree scowled at father and sons while she stroked Bud's damp hair. "You guys had better be nice to me, or I'll go lock myself in the pantry and eat every cookie I can find. And when I'm done with the baked stuff, I'll start on the cake mixes.''

"Looks like you'd better cool it, Ryan.'' Mitch's happiness was so overwhelming he spoke directly from the heart. "You don't want a mother who doesn't share her cookies.''

That brought Bud to full wakefulness. He sat up. "Mother?''

"Yes, mother,'' Mitch said, giving his older son the sternest stare he could manage, to reinforce his decision.

Looking from Bud to Ryan, Mitch decided Bree was a lot more surprised than either boy was. He gave her another quick squeeze, then released her and raked his wet hair back to smooth it. "I guess I got a little ahead of myself again, didn't I? I was going to take you out and impress you with my gentlemanly ways before I talked more about marriage. Guess it's too late for that now." He cleared his throat. "So, will you marry me, Ms. Bailey?"

"You're asking me? Just like that?"

She'd been staring at her scraped legs and ruined sandals. She jumped to her feet, arms outstretched. "Look at me. I've just slid down a mountain. I've been dunked in a mud hole. And I'm dripping like a drowned rat. Where's the romance?"

"You're not going to make this easy for me, are you?"

"Deciding to get married isn't supposed to be easy. It's a big step, Mitch."

"You still want me to court you? After all this?"

Hands fisted on her hips, Brianne made a pretense of being upset. "A few normal dates certainly wouldn't hurt."

He couldn't keep a straight face. "Honey, with the start you and I've had, I doubt anything we do will seem normal from here on."

"Give it a shot." She stood firm, eyebrows raised, waiting.

"Okay. I'll try. Just remember, I haven't done this in a long time."

The boys were edging closer, giving both adults their rapt attention.

Mitch noticed and hesitated before saying, "Ms.

Bailey, would you like to go to dinner and a movie with me?''

"That's better. When?''

"Does it matter?''

"Yes. I think the theater over in Highland is showing a full-length cartoon this weekend. If we get cleaned up and grab an early dinner we can make the first showing.''

"That's your idea of a date?''

"It is now.'' Bree smiled benevolently. The children had been concentrating on the conversation, their little heads snapping right and left like spectators in box seats at a tennis match.

She crouched and opened her arms to them. Bud was first to respond to the invitation for a hug, but Ryan wasn't far behind.

Brianne gave them both an affectionate squeeze. "The last thing I want is for my kids to feel left out.''

"How about me? Where's my hug?'' Mitch asked. "I'm beginning to feel left out.''

"Poor baby.''

Bree stood and patted his cheek, thoroughly enjoying the lost-little-boy look he'd put on for her benefit. If ever there was a man who was all grown up—and then some—it was Mitch Fowler.

No kidding! For her, the hardest part of their supposed courtship was going to be keeping herself from rushing into his arms, pledging her undying love and cutting their dating period very, very short.

Which was further evidence that the Lord had known exactly what He was doing when he'd brought them together like this, she reasoned. They not only had each other, their courtship came complete with two resident chaperons.

At peace, she held out her hands to the children. Bud grasped one. Ryan took the other.

Feeling more content, more maternal, than she'd ever dreamed possible, Brianne said, "Okay kids. Come on. Let's all go home."

A week later, Brianne and Mitch were relaxing in a glider on the porch outside her library and watching the children playing a game of tag.

He put his arm around her shoulders and gave the swing another push with his feet. "So, are you ready to say you'll marry me?"

"You are in a hurry, aren't you?"

"You didn't answer my question."

She smiled him and nodded. "As ready as I'll ever be, I guess."

"Does that mean yes?"

"Yes."

"Good, because I'd hate to have to beg. It's too hard on my ego." He pulled her closer. "In case I haven't told you so in the past five minutes, I love you.''

"I love you, too." She nestled against him and rested her hand on his chest, feeling the steady, rapid beat of his heart. "All three of you."

"Four, counting the dog." Mitch admired his offspring as they chased Barney and each other around the lawn. "They are great kids, aren't they?"

"Sweethearts. Like their daddy."

He kissed the top of her head. "Thanks. Hold that thought. You'll need it when you're standing at the altar pretty soon, saying *I do.*"

"I've been thinking about that. I want the boys to be a part of the ceremony."

"Both of them?"

Bree looked at him, her expression filled with love. "Yes. It's not just for them. It's for me, too. They're my kids, one hundred percent. We're already a family. Leaving them out of our wedding plans is unthinkable."

Mitch couldn't help the wide grin that spread across his face or the warmth coloring his cheeks as his thoughts followed their natural course. "Okay. They can be in the wedding, as long as you don't decide we have to take them with us on our honeymoon, too."

"Well…"

"No, Brianne. No way." He studied her expression carefully, trying to decide whether or not she was serious.

She laughed. "I know. I'm just teasing you. The boys will understand. We'll promise to bring them back some great presents, and they won't hardly notice we're gone."

"You're going to spoil them."

"Sure am." She threaded her fingers through his hair and urged him closer as she whispered, "And I have every intention of spoiling their wonderful daddy, too. Any objections?"

Mitch placed a quick kiss on her lips, then left the swing and retreated across the porch. "Nope. I'll expect you to start spoiling me as soon as you're my wife. Until then, I think I'd better go home."

Laughing gaily, Bree agreed. "I think you're right. We're already the town's favorite scandal."

"I know. I keep reminding folks that a literal act of God is what brought us together. They'll find somebody else to gossip about soon enough."

"It was, wasn't it? And act of God, I mean."

His voice gentled, his eyes misting. "You're not talking about just the storm, are you?"

"No. There was a lot more to it than a little rain. I used to believe in coincidences. No more. There's no way everything that happened to us could have been an accident."

"I agree." Mitch's dark eyes held an unspoken promise. Then he began to smile mischievously. "So, is there anything I can do for you before I leave, Ms. Bailey? Carry you over the threshold? Hug you? Kiss you senseless?"

Bree gazed at him, loving him so much she could hardly contain her elation and marveling at the overwhelming sense of God's presence or of His perfect blessing on their future.

"Soon," she promised, knowing it was true.

"How soon?"

"Very soon." A broad grin lit her face, her cheeks suddenly extra rosy. "Actually, I've picked out my dress already. As soon as we can arrange for the church and find out what dates your pastor has free, we can coordinate everything."

"Good. You're the one who's always organized, so I'll leave all those details up to you. Whatever you decide will be fine with me. I'll take care of our honeymoon plans."

Brianne gave him a quick hug then gazed at him, her blue eyes brimming with love. "Now *that's* romantic."

Epilogue

The day finally arrived.

Brianne could have had the most extravagant wedding Arkansas had ever seen——an enormous sanctuary filled with flowers, a designer gown, a catered reception and a cake big enough to feed all of Little Rock, with plenty left over.

Instead, she'd chosen a simple, fitted white satin dress and an equally simple ceremony in Mitch's home church, surrounded by the majestic beauty of the forested Ozark foothills. Wild maples had already turned bright red and orange, and oaks were beginning to show early fall color.

Bree had filled every corner of the churchyard with pots of chrysanthemums that echoed the rich, natural autumn hues. They made it look as if the whole countryside had purposely been blended into a huge, majestic backdrop painted especially for her nuptials.

At first, she'd thought it would be nice if Ryan escorted her down the aisle, but when Mitch decided to make the eight-year-old his best man, she chose to let Bud do the honors rather than walk to the altar alone.

Finding formal suits to fit the boys necessitated a trip to Batesville. A matching outfit for Bud's freshly shampooed and blow-dried bear was a little harder to come by. Bree finally settled on a black bow tie and red satin cummerbund. In spite of the rough treatment the poor teddy had gotten recently, he looked absolutely elegant, as did his proud owner.

Holding her bouquet in one hand, she stood at the back of the church and reached out to Bud with the other. "You ready, honey?"

"Uh-huh."

"Is your bear ready, too?" It was tucked in the crook of his other arm.

"Uh-huh."

Bud grasped Bree's hand and grinned at her with pure adoration. He'd lost a baby tooth the day before, and the gap made his smile look even more endearing.

"Okay. It's almost time," Bree told him. "See?

There's your daddy and Ryan standing up front. We can go, too, as soon as the right music starts.''

The delay seemed interminable. Her mouth got dry, her palms damp. Even the sight of her beloved Mitch, waiting with the preacher in front of the congregation and smiling encouragement, wasn't enough to calm her jitters. She was doubly glad she had little Bud for company. Worrying about his possible nervousness helped take her mind off the butterflies holding a convention in her stomach.

The boy squeezed her hand and gave it a tug to get her attention. ''Bree?''

''Yes, honey?'' She leaned closer to listen.

''Are you my mama yet?''

''Almost.'' Tears of joy misted her vision. The wedding march began to echo through the small sanctuary, and she stepped forward. ''Just a few more minutes, and I will be.''

''Good,'' Bud whispered. '''Cause my bear's hungry. We really want some more cookies.''

Bree clasped her new husband's arm as they left the church as husband and wife. In spite of the crowd of well-wishers surging around them, they had eyes for only each other.

Mitch covered her hand with his. ''You okay?''

''I will be, as soon as all this is over. I never realized how nervous I'd be.''

"Me, too. I kept worrying that the kids would decide they were tired of being good and start acting up."

"Not a chance. They were little angels. Even Ryan was on his best behavior." Fondness for both children made her smile. "I almost cried when Bud asked me how soon I'd be his mother."

"When was this?"

"While we were waiting to walk down the aisle. The only thing that kept me from bursting into tears was the reason he gave."

Mitch arched an eyebrow. "I'm almost afraid to ask what it was."

Laughing, her eyes sparkling, Bree said, "He told me he and the bear were hungry and they wanted cookies. I guess he figured mothers were the best people to get them from."

"I told you those kids were bright."

"And cute."

"Like their daddy?"

"Yes." Bree cooed the word. "Just like their daddy."

"No second thoughts?"

"None. I still can't believe I'm married, though. I was sure it would never happen. I was never going to have kids, either, and all of a sudden I'm the mother of two. I hope I'm up to the challenge."

"You're perfect. The Lord knew what He was

doing when He threw us together. I'm thankful He made sure we were stuck with each other long enough for both of us to realize what we'd been missing.''

"I just wish it hadn't cost you your cabin."

"Hey, I told you stuff like that doesn't matter."

"I know. I agree, but…"

"No buts. Buildings aren't important. Families are. You, me, the boys, we're all starting over at the same time. We'll make a home wherever we are because we're together."

Given the earnestness of their conversation, he was taken aback by Bree's nervous titter. "What's so funny?"

"Me," she said. "You're being so sweet and serious. I'm ashamed of the notion that just popped into my head. It was really silly."

"What?"

"If I tell you, you'll laugh."

"I hope so. Some of the happiest times I've had lately have been when we've shared a good laugh."

"This has *nothing* to do with my baked chicken recipe," she insisted. "Or with setting pancakes on fire.

"That's a relief." Mitch was already chuckling. He paused long enough to take her in his arms and pull her closer. "Better hurry if you're going to tell me. The photographer's about to have a conniption.

It looks like he wants us to go into the fellowship hall. Probably wants to take pictures of us cutting the cake.''

"Okay. Then let's go."

Mitch wasn't through studying her indefinable expression. "Wait a minute. First, tell me what you were thinking about that made you laugh."

"It wasn't important." Bree tried to break away.

"Then why are you blushing?"

"Blushing? Me?"

"Yes, you. I'm your husband, remember? You can confide in me. You *should* confide in me."

"Well… Okay." Bree raised on tiptoe, cupped her hand around her mouth and whispered in his ear. "All of a sudden, I remembered that old joke about a woman who married a man who already had children because she was too lazy to have them herself."

"That's it? That's all?" Mitch gave her a puzzled look. "What's so funny about that?"

"I think it must have lost something in the translation," Brianne said. "Either that or I'm so uptight I'd laugh at anything right now."

"Maybe. Unless…"

Cocking his head, he bent to speak so that only she could hear. "This is probably not the time or the place to bring this up, Mrs. Fowler, but I have wondered. Are you trying to tell me that you think the boys might need a little sister?''

''Well...'' Bree felt suspended in air, as if her feet had suddenly left the ground. She hadn't brought up the subject of their having children together because she'd been afraid Mitch might change his mind about marrying her if she did. Obviously, he already had all the family he'd ever need. He'd as much as said so. She just wanted...

Her cheeks flamed. Her gaze locked with her husband's. The perceptive look on Mitch's face told her he knew *exactly* what she wanted.

As his expression softened, he leaned down and kissed her, much to the delight of their guests.

When he straightened there was a broad grin on his face. Slipping his arm around Bree's waist, he said, ''I love you, honey, but first things first. Come on. Let's go cut the cake and get our pictures taken.''

''Okay. Then what?'' Bree's heart was pounding so hard and fast she could feel her pulse in her temples without touching them.

''Then, we'll sneak off by ourselves so we can have a nice, long, private talk about you being such a terrible lazybones.''

''I can try to improve,'' she said happily.

Mitch's grin widened. ''Honey,'' he said, ''I'm counting on it.''

* * * * *

Dear Reader,

As you've probably gathered by now, especially if you've read my earlier Love Inspired titles, I love rural life in the Ozark Mountains.

We moved out here in the country to escape, just as Brianne did in my story. Only, we did it for different reasons. We weren't running away from anything, we were running toward it. A city had grown up around us where we'd lived before and our life had gotten too fast-paced and complicated as a result. Yes, wages there were high and jobs were plentiful, but without peace of mind and good physical health, what difference does that make?

So we left. Some of our friends thought we were crazy to follow our dream all the way from Southern California to the backwoods of Arkansas. Others envied us. It took guts and faith to do what we did, but we've never been sorry.

There have been a few interesting surprises along the way, too. I knew I could continue to write no matter where I lived but I'd never imagined how much finding a good country church, a Bible-preaching pastor and dozens of new Christian friends would reshape and refocus my faith.

I had to come here as preparation for the books I'm writing now. I just didn't know it ahead of time!

I invite your letters at P.O. Box 13, Glencoe, AR 72539-0013, e-mails at VALW@centurytel.net or visit my Web site for the latest news, http://www.centurytel.net/valeriewhisenand/.

Blessings,

Valerie Hansen